SILENCE AND SHADOWS

SELECT EDITIONS

This condensation has been created by The Reader's Digest Association Limited by special arrangement with HarperCollins Publishers Ltd.

The original edition of this book was published and copyrighted as follows: SILENCE AND SHADOWS, published at £16.99 by HarperCollins Publishers, © 2001 by James Long. The Author asserts the moral right to be identified as the author of this work. Cover images and front cover/spine of slipcase photomontage (second from left): man: Jonathan Brady*; Gettyone Stone; photomontage by Shark Attack. Author photo on page 159: © Kim Sayer. Slipcase photomontage by Shark Attack. *The publishers have made every effort to trace this photographer.

The Reader's Digest Association Limited,
11 Westferry Circus, Canary Wharf, London E14 4HE.

www.readersdigest.co.uk
ISBN 0-276-42583-9

Printed and bound by GGP Media, Pössneck, Germany

JAMES LONG

SILENCE AND SHADOWS

READER'S DIGEST SELECT EDITIONS
CONDENSED BOOKS DIVISION

Time heals all, so they say. But for one-time rock idol Paddy Kane tragic memories of the wife and son he has lost just won't go away.

Returning to his old passion for archaeology, Paddy immerses himself in the painstaking work of unearthing an Anglo-Saxon burial site, and in doing so realises that it may hold the key to escaping his past.

ONE

He was a tired traveller at the end of his tether, a gaunt shadowed man. He was as alone as it was possible to be and that was his choice. Wales was behind him. It was over for another year but he felt no better for it. Standing by the grave in the wet churchyard, he could hardly believe the person he had been, the man responsible for this headstone with its letters of accusation bitten into the slate.

On the last stage of his journey from the Welsh mountains, Patrick played mind games to keep awake. He ran through the list of the things he must not forget to pack. Tent, sleeping-bag, plate, mug, four-inch trowel. When that developed into its own soporific mantra, he wound down the window, let the damp air wash his face, and turned his attention to the signposts he passed. Village names contain rich pickings for archaeologists.

Archaeology. That was what he had studied, way back when life was simple. That was what he had returned to now. He had decided, in despair, it was easier to deal with those who were long dead.

The sign to the village of Fawler occupied him all the way from Charlbury to the walls of the Blenheim Palace estate. Fawler from 'faig-flor', the term the Anglo-Saxons had used for the mosaics scattered in the ruins left by the vanished Romans. Mosaics were very much on his mind. They were the reason time was tight, the reason he would have to pack in a hurry as soon as he got home.

Right on cue, the sign to Wytchlow flared white for a moment in his headlights and he checked his watch. Twenty past five and dawn was striping the sky to the east—four hours before he was due back here at Wytchlow again, ready to start.

On the very last stretch into Oxford, he blinked abruptly awake. Sleep was claiming him. He turned to his last resort, the radio, and as if there was an evil malignancy presiding over his affairs, a song was ending, a song from that shut-off past, a song he hated deeply.

> *'You can tell the truth to lovers but it's better when you lie.*
> *A puppy's just for Christmas then you leave it out to DIE.'*

'Nam Erewhon there with their infamous punk anthem, "Wedding Vows", requested by . . .'

Patrick's left fist hit the radio so hard that it split the OFF button and the tuning scale behind it into shards of plastic which fell onto the old Peugeot's filthy floor.

In the Cowley Road, a sodden pile of *Woman's Own* had been dumped on his front step—any secondhand value they might once have had washed out by the rain. Two feet away, a sign in the charity shop window scolded in vain: PLEASE DON'T LEAVE DONATED GOODS OUTSIDE. Patrick unlocked the door and the whole pile slumped into his hall so that he had to bulldoze it all back outside with his feet.

This place was not a home, it was just a space with nothing human in it to fight the short-let squalor. There was not enough left of him to turn it into a pleasant place and, anyway, he did not deserve to live in a pleasant place.

He slept for an hour on a harsh mattress that still smelt of some past tenant's spilt beer, then woke himself with a cold shower, not even trying the hot water because he was almost certain that the water heater wouldn't light. He threw what he needed into a bag. In that old life it would all have been there ready, washed and folded for him. Now he had to retrieve his clothes from corners.

There were two letters on the mat. One was an electricity bill, a final demand. The logo on the other envelope said 'Colonic Music' in gold over the silhouette of a broken purple guitar. He tore it open. Inside was a letter, addressed to him care of the company and now forwarded. It started: *Dear Paddy Kane, Can you settle a bet for my brother and me? He says that when you punched . . .*

Patrick crumpled it up, threw it in the bin where the rest of Paddy Kane belonged, and slammed the door of the flat behind him.

All the way out through the north Oxford traffic, retracing his earlier route, fears about the days ahead, his first real test in this new professional role, ballooned into his head. As a student, he had learned the techniques, the terminology, the minutiae. He had then immediately forgotten it all when he had shed the gown and put on the wild clothing of an ever more wild life. Now he was returning to archaeology. For the past two years he had buried himself in stuffy libraries, setting himself a course of intensive reading and picking up the strands of all he had forgotten. If he tried, he might get back to things that had once mattered.

All the money that had once poured through Patrick's fingers had been drunk, snorted and pissed away. The royalties still came in, unwelcome evidence that the songs he wished he'd never sung were still poisoning minds somewhere. Once in a while, he would use those cheques to fill a hole in his bank account. More often, they languished in a drawer until he found a good cause to send them to.

From now on, to sever that link, he intended to survive on a pay packet. He had found what looked like being a steady job with Paradigm Site Check, one of a new breed of companies operating on the profit-making edge of archaeology. His first assignment was one he hadn't been expecting and didn't really want, dumped in his lap by another man's bad luck.

'I know it's a bit early but it's a jolly good opportunity for you to show us what you can do,' John Hescroft had told him on the phone.

He knew straight away what that really meant. There was no time to find anyone else and they didn't want to spend the money. He'd expected to be, at best, number two on a series of digs while he found his feet. Trench supervisor was about his mark, not director. He knew this was beyond his knowledge and his capabilities.

'I'll see you have a good team,' said Hescroft.

A signpost said WYTCHLOW 1 MILE, and the road it pointed down was narrow, twisting between high, banked hedges and soft fields sprouting with an early fuzz of green. A steep rise led up through a dark filter of old woodland towards a clean skyline which showed no sign of the promised village. Then, round a sharp bend, the road was abruptly lined by stone cottages.

No sooner had Patrick registered the outskirts of Wytchlow than a woman burst out from a gateway into his path, looking back the way she'd come, oblivious of him, clearly upset.

He slammed to a complete halt as she banged into his door. She bounced off it and he stared horrified through his open window, shaking with shock, as she staggered to keep her balance. Behind her, blocking the gateway, a middle-aged man in a tweed jacket stood by a sign that said WYTCHLOW PRIMARY SCHOOL. His face was puckered up in distaste and his hand was held up, either warding her off or demanding silence. The woman turned, as if aware of the car for the first time, and bent to look in. Patrick was a foot away from her face.

When Patrick looked into her eyes he was overwhelmed. A flash flood of pure emotion swept through the dry watercourses of his soul. What he saw so shockingly was a perfect double, an identical twin of a girl now locked in his past, the girl with whom he had fallen instantly and completely in love at the age of eighteen.

What he saw first were the eyes—large and dark in a pale face, full lips parted in shock, showing pure white teeth. Her hair was tucked up out of sight under a woollen hat. He stared at her aghast for no more than two seconds. Then he wound up the window and drove away to safety.

He went only a couple of hundred yards, far enough to get out of sight round the corner, then stopped on the edge of an expansive triangle of village green. He stopped to try to put this ambushing genie back in its bottle, but instead the genie just went on swelling in the fresh air.

It was not entirely true to say that this woman was Rachel's double. Someone in their thirties cannot look just like an eighteen-year-old. What this woman with the shining eyes looked exactly like was the Rachel who *would* have been, had her future been in the hands of a kinder lover.

TWO

The road into Wytchlow split and ran down two sides of the triangular village green, flanked by low stone houses, some thatched, some roofed with rough stone tiles. A whitewashed pub was the only building to break the run of warm Cotswold stone. On the third side of the triangle, beyond the war memorial, a field stretched up a gentle slope to an array of old barns along the skyline. The two roads ran off the far corners of the green, curving down past a church on the right and heading into higher ground on the left.

Driving on with part of his brain still locked into a baffled, looped replay of the sight of the woman's face, Patrick took the left-hand lane leading to the field at the far end of the village. As he drove into the tight little square of rough grass, he realised with a sinking heart that he was going to have to stamp his authority on events right away. Tents were going up all over the place, cars parked here and there among them. Only one tent was where it was meant to be, a tattered square marquee of patched canvas, standing beside a pair of mobile lavatories at the field's edge.

Patrick parked hard up against the fence and got out, clutching his clipboard. 'Come over here, everybody, please,' he shouted.

The person nearest to him glanced up for a moment and went back to his guy ropes. He was a crop-haired man with the battered air of a monk from some impoverished order. His forehead was angled back like an Easter Island statue, and round glasses filled his gaunt eye-sockets.

'A moment,' he said in a burred growl. 'I'll just be finishing this.'

'Oh no, you will not,' said Patrick, almost as vehemently as he felt, 'because if you do, you'll just have to take it straight down again.'

'Aren't you just the angry one today?' said the man.

The others were straggling towards him across the grass, a motley crew—a flock searching for a leader. Patrick scanned their faces as they approached, looking hopefully for one who might be the lieutenant he badly needed—the one who would fill the gaps when knowledge or confidence failed him.

The group formed a loose crescent round him. The only one who gave any impression that he had ever been in a field such as this before was a big, tough man of sixty or more—his grey hair bunched back in a ponytail. Across his barrel chest his black T-shirt said TERMINATE WITH EXTREME PREJUDICE, and his arms were covered in tattoos. When Patrick caught his eye, he gave a conspiratorial wink. It was a straw and Patrick grasped at it.

'Have you put your tent up yet?'

The tattooed man laughed and said, 'Not me, mate.'

'OK,' said Patrick to the group. 'Listen to me. I'm Patrick Kane. I'm the director of this dig and the first thing I have to tell you is that you're all going to have to take your tents down again.'

'And why would that be?' asked the Easter Island monk.

'Because you've put them up right over the top of the archaeology,' said Patrick evenly. They shuffled uncomfortably. 'We need the tents close together along the edge of the field over there by the catering tent. Put your cars next to mine at the far end.'

'Couldn't we just dig in between them?' asked a small woman whose blonde hair was much younger than her face and who had bright red lipstick distributed over her teeth as well as her lips. 'It's taken me absolutely ages to put my tent up. I've never camped before, you see.' Her polished, gilt-buckled shoes and white trousers made this explanation unnecessary and there was a guffaw from the tattooed man.

'What's your name?' asked Patrick, looking at his clipboard.

'Gaye,' she said, 'with an e.'

'The answer to your question, Gaye with an e,' said Patrick, 'is no, we can't dig round your tent. You need to move it so that we can start to mark out the trenches. Understood?'

She looked doubtfully towards the edge of the field. 'If that's the catering tent,' she said, 'it's awfully close to the toilets. I think Health and Safety might have something to say about that.'

Patrick ignored her. 'Right,' he continued, 'I've only been working for PSC for a short time so I'm sorry if there are some of you I *should* know and don't. Can I just ask which of you are PSC employees?'

Not a hand was raised.

I don't believe this, Patrick said to himself.

'So, hand up if you're a volunteer,' he said, and it seemed to him that every hand was raised. Just to check, he asked, 'Are there *any* professional archaeologists here?'

The tattooed man lifted a hand the size of a leg of pork. 'I am,' he said. 'Sort of.'

Patrick, feeling suddenly glad for very small mercies, found himself lacking the energy to discover what 'sort of' meant. 'Sorry, I don't know your name,' he said.

'No need to be sorry, Pat,' said the man. 'Be a bit amazing if you did, all things considered, being as how we never met before.'

'So what is it? And by the way, I'm Patrick, not Pat.'

'That's all right, Pat. I'm Dozer.' He was rolling a cigarette with one hand.

'That's another thing,' said Patrick. 'There's to be absolutely no smoking near any of the trenches once we've started.'

'Why is that?' said the monk. 'We are in the open air, after all.'

'What's your name?' asked Patrick, and the man reacted as if the question were a prelude to some sort of punishment.

'Aidan,' he said. 'I was only asking.'

'Tobacco ash mucks up carbon dating,' said Patrick. 'Is there anybody else who's not a volunteer?'

A pallid scarecrow of a boy in a bush hat put up his hand. 'I'm a student,' he said, 'Maxwell Muir. I'm doing this for my course. Fieldwork experience.'

'Right.'

'If we find things,' the boy went on, 'do we get to keep any of them?'

'How long have you been doing your course?' asked Patrick grimly.

'Since October,' said the boy with apparent pride.

'Then you shouldn't need to ask that. Now, the rest of you,' he said, 'how many of you have worked on a dig before?'

Only three.

'Let's see . . .' He looked at his clipboard in search of anything that might give hope. 'Are we all here? I'll just do a head count.'

It came out at sixteen. There were eighteen names on his list. He ran through it and they all answered except for R. Redhead and C. D. Corcoran.

He looked around at them again and found himself exhausted by the unfamiliar experience of speaking more than one sentence to more than one person. He strode away, reaching for his mobile phone. Halfway to the hedge he glanced back to see most of them straggling after him, and shooed them back like a herd of bullocks. He stopped at the corner of the field.

To the north, beyond the hedge, a field of short grass rose gradually over a rounded hill. On the skyline, a cloud shadow swept by and in the sunlight Patrick saw a man, sitting stock-still and hunched up, arms pulling his knees to his chest, staring down at them. Patrick stared back but the man made not the slightest acknowledgment.

The phone rang at the other end and Patrick was through to Hescroft.

'Patrick! How are things going out there? I'm planning to pop out and see you. Few things I want to discuss.'

'Such as?'

'TV,' said Hescroft, putting pleasure into the two syllables. 'Chance of a series if we play our cards right. Do us no end of good.'

'I've got enough on my plate with this dig for now,' Patrick said. 'I'm a bit concerned.'

'I don't think we need get too stirred up about this one, old boy. Pretty slender evidence to mount a Phase Two. Just do the minimum and let the poor bloody builder get on with it.'

That's all I need, thought Patrick grimly. A bent contract. Hescroft's got no interest in finding anything here that would stop the developer putting up his houses. Has he taken a backhander? Probably. John Hescroft was more businessman than archaeologist whatever his CV might say. The outcome of a dig like this could make a huge difference to the value of a building site.

'Is that why I've got such a crap team?' he asked.

'What's the problem, old boy?' Hescroft sounded shocked.

'The problem is that there's nobody here who knows one end of a trowel from the other. They're all volunteers.'

'Archaeology lives off volunteers.'

'Not if it's being done by a professional unit on a paid contract.'

Hescroft retreated. 'They're not *all* volunteers. You've got Phil there, haven't you? Big man. Ponytail, tattoos.'

'He said he was called Dozer.'

'That's him. Done thousands of digs. Knows it backwards.'

'Qualified?'

'School of *life*, old boy. You can't beat experience.'

'Are we paying him?'

'Sort of.'

That phrase again. 'What does that mean?'

Hescroft sounded uncomfortable. 'I'm getting his car fixed for him. It's tax-efficient.'

'Look, John,' said Patrick. 'How am I meant to do the recording? How do I do finds? How do I look after the trenches? I'm going to have to be everywhere at once. If this lot found Pompeii they'd dig right through it and out the other side.'

'Well, hold on there a minute. You've got CD.'

'Seedy?'

'C. D. Corcoran.'

'He's not here yet. Who is he?'

'Best in the business. Smart young Yank doing his doctorate. You'll like him. He takes this incredible bird with him everywhere.'

'Bird?' said Patrick, thinking the last thing he needed was another hanger-on, a girl in tow. Nothing hurt more than the sight of loving couples—nothing, that is, except loving couples with small sons.

Small sons, old enough to walk, young enough to hold hands. They didn't have to be black-haired, blue-eyed images of David. The way they walked, the way they trusted, was enough to pierce Patrick through and through.

He missed most of what Hescroft said next.

'. . . black bird. Great fun.'

Patrick was staring at the entrance to the field, at a man on a huge motorcycle now threading its way through the ruts, and at a black bird, clinging tightly to the rider's shoulder.

A KNOT OF PEOPLE converged round CD and the bird. The bike, a Harley-Davidson, was resting on its stand and CD was pumping the hand of Dozer, on whose shoulder the bird was now standing, cocking its head at each of them in turn.

''Ow long's it been, CD?' Dozer said. 'Where was it last, up the Orinoco?'

CD, a slight figure with thick pebble glasses and a mop of sandy hair, grinned and said with a soft American accent, 'That's right, you old rascal. The Aztec treasure.'

'Yeah, you owe me one for that,' said Dozer, and looked round at the rest. 'Pulled him out of the jaws of a crocodile, I did.'

'Well, yes,' agreed CD, 'but wait until I tell them how you got me *into* its jaws in the first place.'

'Can we save all this for later?' interrupted Patrick. He held out a hand to the American, but the bird hopped onto it instead, digging in its feet to the point of pain.

'I'm Patrick Kane,' he said, and a momentary flicker in CD's eyes alarmed him. 'Can you persuade your crow to go somewhere else?'

'No, no, no, no, no,' said CD. 'Lesson one, never call a raven a crow; they are very easily upset.' He looked at the bird. 'Edgar,' he said, 'come,' and the bird leapt and flapped onto his shoulder.

'That's not a raven or a crow. It's a jackdaw,' objected Gaye.

'I call him Edgar,' said CD, 'therefore he's a raven.'

'What does that mean?' said Gaye, baffled.

'Edgar Allan Poe,' said a smiling elderly man, whose hair was a mixture of grey and ginger. '"Quoth the Raven, 'Nevermore'." Yes?'

She still looked baffled.

'Can we go and talk?' Patrick said to CD, feeling irritation rising again. 'There's a lot to do and nobody much to do it.'

CD blinked amiably. 'That's cool,' he said.

'Just say the word, Pat,' said Dozer. 'I'll get stuck in. Want me to get these tents sorted?'

'Yes, that would help.' The words, 'It's Patrick, not Pat' formed and died on his lips. 'Come on, CD.'

They walked down the edge of the trees until they were alone.

'I've seen you before,' said the American, looking at him curiously.

'Around Oxford?' suggested Patrick, though he knew his recent seclusion made that unlikely.

Then CD stopped, snapped his fingers and said far too loudly, 'Paddy Kane! Sod this Patrick stuff. You're Paddy Kane. My hero. Where's the hair gone?'

'Be quiet,' said Patrick in a fury. 'Keep your voice down. I am *not*. I'm just doing a job here, like you are.'

CD took in the expression on the other man's face. 'OK, Patrick, if you say so,' he said. Then he shrugged. 'So tell me what we have here. A bunch of amateurs?'

'Barely even that,' said Patrick, suddenly anxious to smooth over what had just happened.

'No digger, no site hut, not enough shovels. That's Hescroft. Another contract stolen by undercutting the outfits with proper professional standards. The two of us are just desperate enough to take the job and compromise our immortal archaeological souls.'

That forced a wry grimace out of Patrick. 'The two of us' seemed a generous phrase, and he sensed the possibility of a real friend in this man. 'Why are *you* so desperate?' he said.

'Me? I have a loan to support. I owe the US Treasury more than most Third World countries for my studies. It's OK so long as I go on studying. I only have to pay it back when I get a real job.'

'So your loan just gets bigger and bigger?'

'I'm depending on that. One day it will get so big they'll decide it's a computer error.' CD looked at him. 'What about you? Been dropped in it, right? I guess you haven't done too much yet?'

It could have been a challenging moment with a different man but Patrick found himself letting the mask slip. 'No. I was expecting a gentler start.'

'OK, buddy. Don't sweat it. I can help here.'

'You should be the director, not me.'

CD laughed. 'You're staff. Hescroft has to pay you anyway. I'm freelance. He doesn't want to shell out Dig Director dollars to me. I'm here for the beer money.'

They talked until they saw the tents had been put in the proper places. Then Dozer walked over to them. CD welcomed him with a grin. 'Three of us against the world, right, Dozer?'

'Yeah, just like that time in Siberia, mate. 'Ere, Pat, who's doing grub?'

Patrick looked at the clipboard. 'It doesn't say. All it says here is they've made arrangements.'

'Yeah, well, it's all in there,' said Dozer, nodding at the marquee. 'Boxes of this and that. There's gas rings there an' all. Just needs somebody to put it together. Anyway, there's something else you've got to worry about first. Trowels. Absence of.'

'How would it be if I give them the standard trowel lecture?' suggested CD, and Patrick agreed gratefully without the faintest idea what that was.

CD gathered the volunteers round him on the grass.

'OK, listen up,' he said. 'In a minute the director will be briefing you about the dig itself, but first off it falls to me to do a bit of the basic stuff. Hands up those of you who have a trowel with you?'

What they produced ranged from huge pointing trowels, still encrusted with old mortar, to tiny curved things of bent, coloured tin intended for brief flirtations with window boxes. CD held up his own. 'This is the only trowel to have. It's a four-inch WHS pointing trowel and nothing else will do.'

'And why do you say that?' said Aidan, the Easter Island monk.

'Because it has a forged blade and handle that are all of a piece,' replied CD equably.

'Eighteen quid they wanted for one of those,' said Aidan, scowling. 'I got mine at B&Q for three pounds ninety-nine.'

'This is not just a trowel,' replied CD. 'It is an extension of your arm and your arm is an extension of your brain. This is what tells you when you've found the finest of fine differences in the soil. Every little bit of information this blade meets goes on the fast track to intellectual processing. This is the blade that cannot lie.'

'And me thinking it was just a thing for shovelling dirt,' said Aidan.

'Soil, please,' said CD, 'never dirt. Soil has a million subtle varieties. You will form a deep bond with the soil. You will learn to taste it. Literally. When you find a piece of something that could be a pot or could be a rock, you will learn to put it in your mouth and see how it tastes because the mouth is the most sensitive organ.'

'That's disgusting,' said the blonde woman with the lipstick. 'I shan't be doing that.'

A frightened-looking, elderly woman at the back held up a very shiny trowel. 'I say,' she said, 'mine's a WHS but it's eight-inch not four. Will that do?'

'Well now, let's see,' CD said. 'In many parts of the world where you need something long enough to fend off the things that come out and bite that would do very well indeed. Here, I'm sorry to tell you, it is very definitely far too big.' CD opened a rucksack and started to bring out trowels. 'I guess I've got enough here to go round. Five pounds to hire one. Fifteen to buy.'

'They're old,' said Aidan. 'That's daylight robbery.'

'Yup,' agreed CD, 'I have a Harley-Davidson and a hungry raven to support. Gather round afterwards and shower money into my hands, but first we have to talk about mattocks.' He paused and looked around him. 'Today we will be deturfing. That is unglorified gardening. You will hate it. You will be using spades, shovels and mattocks to get rid of the topsoil and—'

Aidan raised a hand. 'I just wanted to ask, isn't it a bit easy to break things with a mattock?'

'That just about hits it on the head,' said CD. 'It is extremely easy to break things with a mattock. You might even say that breaking things is the whole point of a mattock, its *raison d'être*.'

'But we don't want to break things we might find, surely?'

'OK, time for one of CD's blinding insights, folks. Pay close attention here.' He cleared his throat. 'Most everything that's in the ground's been broken for a couple of thousand years already. Hit it with a mattock and you don't do it much more harm than history already did. Break nothing, find nothing. Get good with your mattock and know when to reach for your trowel. Anyway, it's only Roman crap we're looking for here. Far too easy. I'm an Anglo-Saxon man myself, stains in the soil. At this point I'll hand over to the director so he can tell you exactly why we're here.'

There was a moment of expectant silence before Patrick realised they were all looking at him. 'Um, there's a developer called . . .' He looked at his clipboard. '. . . Roger Little who has applied for planning permission to build houses on this site. There was some historical evidence of tesserae being picked up in the plough-soil here.' He saw that most of their faces were blank. 'That's pieces of Roman mosaic flooring. They've done a geophysical survey and there is evidence of a rectangular structure in the middle of the field. We have to find out whether there is anything important here before the building goes ahead. You can all have an hour off to get sorted out while we mark out the trenches, then we'll get stuck in.'

Patrick took CD and Dozer into the field with tapes, pegs and a mallet, and they marked out the first trench from the information in the geophysical print-out. While the other two were taping it, he walked away to the far corner to establish the line of the second trench and when he looked up he saw the watching man was up there on the hillside again.

As Patrick bent to push in a peg, his keen ears caught a shred of familiar words passing between CD and Dozer: '". . . Man's intended for deceiving—that's why Adam met the snake."'

He looked up at once, indignantly, and caught Dozer looking towards him, and CD guiltily looking away. Guessing at what had just passed between them, he felt a hot wash of betrayal.

When they came over to join him, his first instinct was to make an excuse and walk away, but he knew it had to be faced.

'Hey, Pat,' said Dozer, 'I thought—'

'No, me first,' Patrick said. 'I heard that and I can guess the rest. I want you to know that I just don't need it, right? You may think it's funny or something, but it's not.'

'I don't think it's funny,' said Dozer, 'and it ain't anything to be ashamed of, chum. You were one of the greats.'

'You wrote the words that made us all think,' said CD.

'No, no. You know nothing about it,' said Patrick. 'It's buried. It's in the past and I've got the right to leave it there. It has nothing to do with me now. I'm asking you both to keep it to yourselves.'

Dozer reached out and squeezed his shoulder. 'All right, Pat, whatever you say,' and Patrick was, for the first time, profoundly grateful he'd said Pat, fearing he might have said Paddy.

'Finish off this one, would you?' he said, looking at the trench and trying to keep his voice level. 'I'll go and see about the cooking.'

It was out of the frying pan into the fire. As he walked down towards the food tent, he could see there was someone inside. When he went through the flap, he collided for the second time with that scalding reminder of his past, the woman from the road.

PADDY KANE HAD WRITTEN 'Wedding Vows' in a drunken rage and almost immediately wished he hadn't. It became the single song for which his bawdy, violent band was best remembered and the main marker of the breakdown of his life. The story of how he wrote it became a punk rock legend in its own right.

This was the way it happened. Paddy Kane was delivered home one morning by a Colonic Music limo straight from Heathrow after a Frankfurt concert. He slammed in through the front door of his Georgian house near Marlow, furious that the crude nude figure he had sprayed on the front wall had been covered up in his absence. Rachel was too scared of him by this time to have it removed but she had compromised by concealing it behind a climbing rose.

Benny, the driver, was a Colonic Music faithful who could be relied on not to give away the story of the Marlow house, the house that didn't exist, or the wife and son, who didn't exist either. Benny was Paddy's confidant.

'What's up, Pat?' Benny said on the way back, because he alone in the company never called him Paddy. 'Bad gig?'

'I'm fucked,' the star said, and Benny knew what he meant.

They had dropped off Vic Bogart, Colonic's boss, first and Benny had heard every word he'd said. 'Paddy boy, the rags are sniffing round. We got to slide a little skirt into the picture, kid.'

'There's . . . there's Rache.' Paddy's voice had been slurred.

'Yeah, there's your contract too. I'm talking glamour here, not childhood sweetheart.'

When Bogart got out, Benny had taken a risk. 'You don't have to do what he says. Tell him to stuff himself. Make that little girl of yours happy. What is it stops you, Pat? On stage you're a demon. You come off and you let these old men push you around. You got to learn to handle them.'

There was a silence from the back. Benny was worried because he knew Bogart's plan. Paddy Kane was on the ragged edge. Booze him up, hand out the powder and he'd blow away Rachel all by himself. When she'd gone, the manner of her going could be a story—if it helped sell records. Benny didn't want that. He'd liked young Pat Kane when he'd first met him. Kane was intelligent, Kane was nice, Kane cared. Before they pushed the poison into him.

'You don't have to do it,' he said again as he held the limo door open. 'You're worth a cartload of money to them. Tell them to stuff themselves and they'll have to listen.'

It was too late. Paddy lurched in through the front door, ready to direct his vengeance in an entirely inappropriate direction.

He'd been enjoying student life and she'd just started teacher training, when he'd met Rachel at a dance. They'd both been far too young, two eighteen-year-olds who had married a year later in a vague haze of sweetness with circlets of daisies in their hair. Then in his final year of archaeology, playing in his student band at a town-centre pub, a scout had heard Patrick sing, and the lyrics he'd written, and had noticed the way, when Pat moved, every female eye followed. Pat had graduated with a contract already signed.

The money men of Colonic Music had seen how Pat's talent for words could be tuned to a new cutting edge. They'd started to channel him in their direction, and his slender reserves of wisdom and experience had not been enough to keep him straight. His music had changed to a harsher beat. Every big cheque had made it harder to say they were wrong. Rachel's invisibility had been part of the deal—a madness foisted on him that became madder still when David was born. Rachel had kept praying he would draw a line. When that seemed increasingly unlikely, she put her efforts into making a nest for their son, and the gulf between Rachel and Pat grew daily wider.

When Benny dropped him off in his wild, sleepless, fuelled-up state, Paddy had no idea that it was Monday and that, on Mondays, Rachel helped out at David's kindergarten. The house into which he staggered was silent and that wound him up even tighter. When shouting failed to produce any sign of Rachel, he took a thick black felt-tip pen and began to write all across the white kitchen wall, and what he wrote was the first and final draft of 'Wedding Vows'.

An hour later, as the alcohol loosened its hold, it started to dawn on him that this might be a mistake. Finding a pot of white paint in the garage, he covered the wall in obliterating emulsion.

When Rachel and David came home at lunchtime, he was quiet, somewhere deep inside himself. Rachel questioned him about the fresh paint but he wouldn't reply. She left him alone while David sat on his knee for much of the afternoon, content to be there even when his father fell asleep. Rachel put David to bed and later, when she had cooked supper, woke Paddy as one might approach an unexploded bomb.

It was halfway through a silent meal that she looked past his shadowed, staring eyes and saw dark shapes developing through the drying paint on the wall behind. She read the lyrics with growing anguish.

A wife is there for leaving. Marriage vows are made to break.
Man's intended for deceiving—that's why Adam met the snake.
Adultery's for adults, faithful's just for fools.
Monogamy's monotonous, even rulers break the rules.
You can tell the truth to lovers but it's better when you lie.
A puppy's just for Christmas then you leave it out to DIE.

Rachel's brother called in on his way to a party that evening, found his sister distraught and Paddy asleep, and copied the words down when Rachel wasn't looking, thinking—but not daring to say—that they were quite good. A girl he was trying to impress at the party that night took them out of his pocket when he fell asleep on her bed later and told the *Sun*. The newspaper printed every word of the song. The band's keyboard player wrote the music the very next morning and Paddy walked in late to a rehearsal studio to find his monster had taken living, breathing shape.

From that moment, Rachel lost her faith that Paddy would one day be Pat again—the Pat she had met and loved. He had stripped the surviving fragments of joy out of her so that what was left was no longer anything like the girl bride with the daisies in her hair.

Pat turned himself more and more into Paddy, a man with no need for responsibility, a man drawn not to sweet, quiet girls but to wild, fierce women who could match him drink for drink, drug for drug. Vic Bogart and his PR polished the legend of the wild man and his life on the road with the band. Paddy did not know then that there is a price for everything, and it was only when the bill came, on a sunny afternoon in Perugia, that he recoiled. He abruptly left the band, cut his extravagant, dyed hair, abandoned his extravagant, dyed life and became Patrick, puritan, isolated Patrick, and tried to get back to a worthwhile point in his life, to do some growing up.

IN THE CATERING TENT, the woman who had brought back memories of Rachel gave a little cry of shock as a tray was knocked out of her hands so that slices of cheese fell all over the grass.

'Oh, sorry,' she said, dropping to her knees and scooping up the cheese.

'I didn't know you were there,' Patrick said.

'Well, I was hoping you hadn't done it on purpose,' she said, giving him a quick grin. 'It's only grass. I don't suppose it matters.'

He stood there immobilised and tongue-tied.

'You can help me if you like,' she said. 'I don't want the boss to see me messing up the lunch before I've even got started.'

He knelt next to her and began to pick up the slices of Cheddar.

'I only told them I could do catering because I wanted to be on the dig. Have you met the director yet?'

'Who?' said Patrick, who had been lost in the sound of her voice without really taking in her words.

'The director.'

'Oh no. Well yes, I'm him.'

'You're . . .?' Horrified, she scrambled to her feet. 'Oh God, I'm sorry, I didn't realise. You must think I'm really stupid. I'm Bobby Redhead,' she said, holding out a hand.

'I'm er . . . I'm Patrick,' and he left out the Kane which seemed too dangerous in combination.

'Look, don't mind what I said, I *can* do the catering really.'

He didn't care in the slightest whether she could or couldn't.

'I saw you earlier, didn't I?' he said. 'I was in my car. You were having a row with somebody at the school.'

'Oh, was that you too? I'm sorry. I was a bit upset.'

Patrick tried to be professional. 'Do you have enough gas rings to do hot food in the evenings?' He looked around to break the gravitational pull of those eyes. 'They'll need a hot meal at the end of the day.'

'I thought I'd get it ready at home. Then I can bring it over and reheat it a bit.'

'How far away is home?'

She lifted the flap of the tent. 'Over there. Highbury Farm.'

Two fields away, a jumble of old stone buildings sat in a dip. A roof of lichened stone tiles branched and sprouted into dormers and cross-wings. Two barns formed the other edges of an open square and reinforced the message of the tractor in the yard. This was a working place.

'How much do you farm?'

'Not much—sixty acres.'

'This wasn't your field, was it?'

Her tone changed sharply. 'I wouldn't have sold it if it had been. It went with the old wood and the estate. I didn't even know it was up for sale when Little wriggled in and bought it.'

'You don't approve of this man Little, then?'

'I don't trust Roger Little and I certainly don't approve of Roger Little, no. The very best thing that could happen to Wytchlow right now would be for us to find something so important that he couldn't build his damned houses at all.'

'That doesn't happen too often, I'm afraid,' said Patrick.

'We can but hope.'

'Do you farm by yourself?'

'No, no. It's me and Joe.'

Well, of course there would be a Joe.

From outside the tent, a bass voice boomed, 'Oy, Pat.'

Patrick ducked back out to daylight and safety.

Dozer stood there jerking a thumb at a man standing talking to CD. 'Builder's 'ere,' he said.

Roger Little was a huge man with a pugnacious jaw and a Birmingham accent who looked elsewhere when he talked, as if he couldn't be bothered with you.

'You're not started yet, then?' were his first words.

'We've just marked out the trenches.'

'Look, time is money, right? Your man—what's he called? Heskin? He said this wouldn't take long.'

'That depends what we find. We're deturfing today and—'

'By hand? For Christ's sake, I'll get a machine up here.'

Normally, that would have been a welcome offer.

'No, thanks,' said Patrick. 'We can do it better by hand.'

Little stared around him at the diggers. 'This lot don't look like they've ever done a full day's work in their lives.'

CD laughed. 'Appearances can be deceptive.' With its head cocked on one side, the bird, perched on his shoulder, inspected the builder. 'You see Vera over there?' He pointed at the wispy woman who'd had the eight-inch trowel. 'She found tomb two eighteen in the Valley of the Kings. Dug it all by herself, shifted four hundred cubic metres of sand single-handed in eighteen days.' He stepped closer to Little and lowered his voice. Then there's Dozer here. Former President of the UK Hell's Angels. I've seen him lift a two-hundred-pound sarsen stone with one hand.'

'Pleased to meet you, Mr Small,' said Dozer, holding out a hand. Little gave a gasp as his own hand disappeared completely inside it, and seemed to decide not to argue about his name.

'Well, why don't I get a digger up here anyway?' he said. 'I'll have a man for you any time you want to use it.'

'Nah, just leave the keys. I'm trained,' said Dozer.

In the remaining two hours before lunch they cut the edges of one trench and took the turf off half of it. The team rapidly divided into the stalwarts and the complainers, led by Gaye, for whom nothing was ever right. She had some justification. The mattocks had splintery wooden handles, the spades had blunt blades, and out of ten wheelbarrows only two did not suffer from some combination of soft tyres, bent axles and missing bolts.

Then there was Maxwell, the student. Maxwell kept finding things. As every turf was hacked and levered out, Maxwell, scarlet eruptions scattered across an otherwise chalky face, would kneel to scan the exposed surface as if the rim of the Holy Grail might well be poking through it. Work in the immediate vicinity would then have to stop while he levered a small piece of stone from the earth and took it excitedly to show Patrick and CD. The first, second and third times, they took the trouble to look at his find closely, explain that it was natural and send him back to work with encouraging noises. The fourth time, CD held it up to the bird, which pecked at it and chattered.

'What do you reckon, Edgar?' said CD. 'Geology?'

Edgar lifted his tail and excreted.

'Yup,' said CD. 'Thought so. Geology.'

'What does that mean, geology?' said Maxwell.

'Rock,' said CD. 'Archaeology means things, geology means rock.'

The fifth time, CD took the proffered stone and without even looking at it, hurled it over the hedge.

'That could have been important,' protested Maxwell, aghast.

'Yup,' said CD. 'I guess we'll never know.'

By the time they broke for lunch, CD had managed to establish a position with the others that Patrick deeply envied, an air of effortless expertise that the humour helped. Dozer, too, had the attention and respect of the rest, but Patrick knew that he himself was far more of a mystery.

'Clear up your loose,' shouted CD when Patrick called lunch break.

'And what does that mean?' said Aidan, pushing his glasses firmly back into his eye-sockets with one finger as he straightened up.

'Get rid of the loose earth, put your tools on the ground, tip the barrows over to cover them.'

'Why don't we leave them where they are?' objected Aidan.

'OK,' said CD wearily, 'gather round for lesson two in CD's insights series.'

They all came towards him. He looked at them benevolently.

'You do it because I say so, and to get into practice for when it matters, because when you get down to the exciting stuff, if you leave the trench full of loose earth and it rains, then all you've got when you come back is mud, and we don't like mud because it washes the evidence all over the goddamn floor.'

‘So we put the barrows over the tools to keep them dry?’

‘No. You put the barrows over the tools because if you step on a mattock, I don’t want to get sued.’

They sat on the grass outside the catering tent, eating doorstep sandwiches of cheese and pickle. The other diggers looked exhausted by their morning’s work and seemed too reticent to join CD, Patrick and Dozer. Patrick knew he should be making the effort to get to know his crew but he couldn’t summon up the energy. Instead, he sat in his own reverie while CD and Dozer spun ever more apocryphal tales to each other of their imaginary exploits together. Patrick watched Bobby as she moved in and out of the tent. Her dark woollen cap made her cheeks seem startlingly pale.

Gaye came over to him at a moment when he was miles away.

‘You’ll have to do something. We really can’t be expected to put up with it,’ she said, indignantly. ‘They’re revolting.’

‘What are?’

‘The . . . facilities. Those things.’ She pointed at the loos. ‘You can *see*.’

‘What can you see?’

‘Everything. It’s all just . . . well, lying there. It’s repulsive.’

‘It’s all right. That’s how they work. They’re full of special chemicals that neutralise it all. It’s perfectly healthy. You don’t have to look.’

CD put on a wolfish smile. ‘I like looking in them,’ he said. ‘It’s inspirational, it’s ever-changing. The colours are fascinating. You wait until we have curry. Beef vindaloo is best. After that . . .’

Gaye had gone. She was replaced immediately by spotty Maxwell.

‘I’ve been talking to the others,’ he said. ‘We all want to know when we’re going to start *finding* things.’

‘Really?’ said CD. Edgar hopped off his shoulder and settled on Maxwell’s head. Maxwell tried to bat the bird away but it dug its claws into the boy’s scalp.

‘Keep still and he won’t hurt you,’ said CD amiably. The jackdaw spread its wings for balance and stood there swaying like a heraldic crest on a knight’s helmet. ‘Now tell me, Maxwell,’ CD went on, ‘I guess you've seen the Indiana Jones movies.'

'Well, yes,' said Maxwell incautiously, 'I have, all of them.'

'And you just can't wait to find the secret chamber with the treasure in it.'

'Oh no, I know it's not going to be like that but I just—'

'Come with me.' CD stood up and the bird flew back to his shoulder. 'Over here, everybody. CD's insights number three.'

He led them to the plastic lavatories, with Gaye lagging well behind, and opened the door of the first of the pair.

'OK, Maxwell,' he said. 'Stick your head down there.'

'Where?' said the boy, appalled.

'Bottom left, down by the floor. Read me what it says.'

Patrick had tagged along to see what CD was up to. The stench was terrible.

Maxwell, crouched and twisted so that his head was distressingly close to the moulded plastic lavatory bowl, sounded as if he was gagging as he read the inscription: 'The Polyjohn Manufacturing Company, Wilmington, Indiana. US patent number seven five—'

'Stop right there. That's enough. You can come out now.'

Maxwell uncoiled himself rapidly.

'Listen up, everybody,' said CD. 'Patrick has asked me to tell you about *finds*.' Patrick hadn't done any such thing but was profoundly grateful that the American was sensitive to his authority. 'Finds are nice,' CD drawled. 'Finds are fun, but mostly finds are useful because finds help give us *dates*. Information is what we are looking for. If we find things we do not rush to dig them up. Oh no. We come and tell teacher and we are very, very careful to leave our find exactly where it is.'

Aidan cleared his throat. 'And perhaps you could tell us why exactly this young man had to stick his head down there so you could tell us that?'

CD laughed. 'Young Maxwell would like to be Harrison Ford and he's kinda hoping the Ark of the Covenant is round here somewhere. As you know, archaeology Indiana Jones-style is all about grabbing the treasure, escaping in a hail of bullets and to hell with recording the context.' He slapped the side of the blue plastic box. 'Well, this is the Indiana John, folks, and that's as close as you're ever going to get.' He looked at Patrick, and tapped his watch.

Patrick nodded. 'Back to work, folks. Tea break at three thirty.'

As they straggled off, Patrick heard Aidan grumbling to Maxwell. 'The thing that worries me is how he *knew* that name was down there.'

Because there is very little justice in life, it was Maxwell who made the big find later that afternoon.

THE YELL BROUGHT all the diggers rushing to the boy who had uttered it. It was too early for a find, they were still taking off the turf, but Maxwell had not followed the conventional, slow, patient ways of archaeology; Maxwell had dug his very own hole—a small square pit a foot and a half deep with coloured fragments gleaming at its bottom. Piled at the edge of the trench were what Maxwell had taken out of his pit, a small stack of dirty slabs.

Patrick pushed his way through the cluster of craning diggers. 'What's happened here?' he demanded.

'Mosaic tiles. You know, your tesser things. See? I've found a floor,' said Maxwell, pleased as punch and failing to pick up any warning from Patrick's tone.

Patrick looked at the hole and the pile beside it, unable to believe that one overgrown teenager could do so much damage.

CD and Dozer arrived at a run and gazed into Maxwell's hole.

'You took those out?' Patrick pointed at the dirty pile of slabs.

'Yup, and just look what was hiding under them.'

'You've removed a destruction layer, you little pillock. Roman roof tiles. You've dug right through the context. You've destroyed information. We need to know *how* this roof collapsed. You said you were an archaeology student, for God's sake. Haven't you learned *anything* yet?'

'I'm only a first year.' Maxwell blinked at him. 'I have found a floor, haven't I?'

It was true that at the bottom of that unforgivable hole there was a glint of rich colour, red and white and yellow, where a scatter of mosaic fragments poked through the moist earth.

'We told you. We're not here to find things. We're here to untangle the story of this place, slowly and carefully—not like a bloody bulldozer.' Patrick was on the verge of telling Maxwell to pack his tent when he saw a small, shining tear appear at the corner of the boy's eye. The part of him that could no longer bear to cause pain revolted. 'Oh, sod it,' he said. 'CD, give them a thorough lecture about contexts, will you?'

'OK,' said CD wearily. 'What is a context anyone?'

The older man with gingery grey hair answered. 'It's the position of a find on a site and its stratigraphic relationship to its immediate surroundings.'

CD blinked. 'I guess that's about the perfect textbook answer.'

Patrick reached for his list. 'I'm sorry, you are?'

'Peter Knight,' said the man.

'And you are Emeritus Professor of Archaeology at which university?' said CD.

Peter laughed. 'No such luck, I'm afraid. I've been a bit of a bookworm all my life. Lots of theory, not much practice. '

Aidan frowned. 'I have to say that explanation was as much use to me as a stepladder in a sandstorm.'

'OK. Well in plain language a context is a layer,' said CD. 'A layer of time. Suppose it's a ditch, then the surface of the ditch is a context. Supposing the ditch got itself filled in to halfway up, then that fill and anything that's in it is a context. When you're digging one context, whatever's sticking up out of the next one, even if it's the missing treasure of Eldorado, you don't disturb it until you've removed and recorded the whole of that context. Ever. Right?'

A rising growl made Patrick look towards the road. A large yellow digger crawled into view from behind the trees and turned to sway its way into the field. Roger Little walked in behind it with a proprietorial swagger. At that moment, Patrick caught a movement out of the corner of his eye. He saw the watcher was on the hill again, nearer now. For the first time, Patrick could make him out, a man of middle age, powerfully built—an outdoors man in a dun-coloured shirt and heavy, working trousers. As Little strode into view, the man on the hill made an abrupt lateral gesture with his arm, as if warding off something in disgust, and turned away.

'How are you getting on?' said Little as he arrived.

'Fine.'

'Waste of time. There's nothing here. Never was.'

A more experienced man might have kept quiet but Patrick found himself blessing young Maxwell for the first time that afternoon.

'There is. We've already found it. A Roman floor by the look of it.'

'Go on with you. Where?'

'There, see?'

Little looked into the hole for an uncomfortably long time.

'Funny way to dig a hole,' he said. 'Straight down like that. I thought you lot did things more carefully.'

'That's what we call a sondage,' said CD. 'Used for getting us a baseline resistivity check when the barometric pressure variation might invalidate the groundline reading.'

Little clearly had no idea what the American was talking about, but then nor did Patrick and nor did CD.

'So what happens next?' said the builder grumpily.

'We follow the lines of the geophysical survey,' Patrick told him. 'This shows up as a corner, so it looks like it confirms the indications that what we might have here is a rectangular structure.'

Little squinted around the field. 'How far does it go?'

Patrick remembered the rough shape on the print-out. 'I'll pace it out,' he said. He walked twenty paces diagonally towards the far hedge then turned at right angles and took twelve more. Little stood watching him as he completed the rectangle and came back.

'Could be worse. Maybe I could build round it. Leave it as a garden.' The builder sniffed and squinted up at the clouds. 'Best be off, I've got work to do. There's going to be a lot of rain.'

He was right. At half past four, an icy, drenching rain first washed the emerging layer of Roman roof tiles brilliantly clean, then filled the trench with an obliterating layer of muddy water.

The catering tent became a haven for the diggers as they huddled together at the rickety table inside, trying to avoid the dribbles leaking through the ancient canvas seams.

Gaye complained loudly. 'You can't expect us to sleep in the tents in this, surely? Isn't there a guesthouse or something?'

CD stuck his head out of the flap. 'Nothing wrong with this. Just a little local precipitation. That's all.'

Gaye's tent blew away at five o'clock, dragged across the grass by the rising wind. Dozer guffawed loudly at the sight, then looked at her stricken face and went out into the downpour to retrieve it and put in all the extra tent pegs that she had left out.

At five forty-five the old marquee gave up the struggle, letting water pour in simultaneously in a dozen new places at once. Patrick had no clear idea what to do, but then help came from an unexpected quarter. A van drove into the field entrance and its owner ran across to the diggers.

'I've got some dry sheds you can all sleep in at my yard,' said Roger Little. 'I suppose I'm responsible for you one way and another. Get your gear and pile in.'

There was a murmur of relief all round.

'OK,' Patrick said to Little. 'Thanks.'

They piled into the back of the van and were driven through the village to what had once been a farmyard. Only one barn survived and around it stood a cluster of small, square industrial units. Little unlocked one. It was large enough for all of them and blessedly dry.

'What are you doing about grub?' said Little.

'Bobby's cooking it. The woman from Highbury Farm.'

'Oh, her,' said Little. 'She's off her head, that woman. Tell you what: I'll get the grub brought over here, shall I? One of my blokes can pick you all up in the morning.'

'He's changed his attitude,' Patrick remarked to CD when the builder left them. 'I never expected any help from that quarter.'

CD gave him a delphic look. 'I guess,' he said. 'Anyway, I'm not too good on concrete, I might just walk back down there later on and sleep in that nice soft mud.'

But the American's intentions were fatally undermined by the dozen litre bottles of rough red wine that arrived unexpectedly with the food and allowed them all to sleep on that hard floor.

When Patrick woke the next morning, the shed looked like a refugee camp, an untidy sprawl of bodies, heads resting on shoulders of people who had been perfect strangers the day before. He remembered raucous singing late into the night and CD filling his plastic mug repeatedly for him in a vain attempt to get him to join in. When the party got to take-off point, horribly like old times, he had retreated into a corner, shunning the friendship and especially the songs.

His watch said 8.05. He wriggled out of his sleeping-bag and decided to walk to the field. He was halfway to the village when a beaten-up Land Rover passed him going fast the other way, braked, turned and came back to him. Bobby jumped out and his heart did a treacherous cartwheel.

'Get in,' Bobby said. 'You won't believe this. I'm so sorry. I should never have let it happen.'

'What? What's happened?'

She was on the verge of tears. 'Just get in.'

They were at the field in two minutes. The digger was standing in the middle of a sea of mud. Desecration had taken place. A huge rectangle of grass had been carved away to two feet or more below the surface, and Patrick knew with appalling certainty that the hole covered the whole area he had so obligingly paced out for Roger Little the day before.

'I slept through it,' Bobby said angrily.

'I'm an idiot,' said Patrick. 'Why didn't I stay with the tents?'

They stared at it in silence for a few moments.

'Shall we go and see him? I know where he lives,' said Bobby.

'You mean Little?'

'Of course I mean Little. Who else would I mean?'

'Well, what would I say?' He couldn't bear the way she was looking at him as if he had let her down. 'Yes,' he said. 'Sure. You bet.'

Little was coming out of his garage as they drove into his yard. He stopped and raised his eyebrows at the style of their arrival. Bobby was out of the Land Rover almost before it stopped, Patrick following her because he had no choice, propelled headlong into a confrontation for which he was not ready.

'What you've done is inexcusable,' said Bobby.

'What I've done?' said Little in mock astonishment.

'You know bloody well what I'm talking about.'

'I don't think I do and I don't like being addressed like that.'

'You dug up the field.'

'What, someone's dug it up, have they? You didn't leave the keys in the digger, did you? With all the kids around here? I hope they haven't done any damage.'

'Kids who cart all the earth away?' said Bobby. 'Do you know what you've destroyed?'

'You be careful what you say,' said Little. 'You could get sued for saying things like that.'

What happened next came as a complete surprise to Patrick, who felt himself taken over as if possessed by another voice, another body. Shaking with the effects of a flood of adrenaline born from fury, he moved in between Bobby and the builder, boring into Little's personal space and pushing him back towards his door with the force of his words and the ready-to-snap tension vividly evident in every fibre of his body.

'Listen to me, you,' he said. 'Who else stands to benefit from wiping out that site, eh? Who else knew exactly which bit to destroy? Do you think anybody's going to believe it wasn't you?' His voice was getting louder. 'You took us for suckers, didn't you? Getting us out of the way? Well, if you think you're going to get your planning permission now, you've got another think coming.'

They had reached the house, Little giving ground backwards all the way, and finally the builder turned quickly, opened his door and stepped inside.

'You can't talk to me like that,' he said through the closing gap. 'Get off my land.'

In the Land Rover, heading back to the field, Bobby said, 'You were fantastic,' but all Patrick could do, instead of basking in the glow of her approval, was to sit there appalled by the knowledge that the old Paddy still lurked inside him, waiting for the slightest chance to get out.

Three

In the pub that night, an ancient, wheezing stranger in a greasy cloth cap stuck his face close to Patrick's and opined that it wasn't Friday, jabbing him in the arm for emphasis and cackling with the mysterious humour of it. It was the fourth or fifth time that one of the locals had mentioned that it wasn't Friday, nodding as they did so towards the far end of the bar where a stool, a guitar and a mike stand were set up on a platform.

Every few seconds the door would open, letting in cold, wet air and cold, wet villagers who would also give their opinion that it wasn't Friday, and sometimes seek confirmation from the strangers huddled by the radiator in the corner. There had been no shortage of opinions expressed that day. By the time they all crowded into the pub that evening, Patrick felt he'd heard enough to last a lifetime.

Dozer's had been the most painful and the most straightforward.

'He'll get away with it, won't he? Must 'ave mates on the planning committee or he wouldn't have risked chucking his cash at that field in the first place. If we can't prove it was 'im, they'll just roll over and let him tickle their tummies.'

CD had blamed himself. 'That's why I planned to go back and sleep down there,' he said. 'I shouldn't have drunk that wine.'

Gaye was looking on the bright side. 'Does that mean we can all go home now?' she asked. 'I could certainly do with a good bath.'

Hescroft had been the worst, pre-empting Patrick by turning up at the field while Patrick had still been trying to get him on his mobile. Hescroft's opinions had been uncompromising. Patrick had shown an extraordinary lack of judgment in leaving the site to the mercy of hooligans. There was very little hope of taking any effective action against Little without hard evidence. Anyway, what made Patrick so sure it *was* Little? It could have been anyone. After all, they *had* left the key in the digger, which was a childish mistake. 'What do I do? Kenny Camden, the series producer, is coming to see me tomorrow,' Hescroft had said. 'What on earth am I going to tell him?'

'Tell him that we didn't find anything. What do I do with all my diggers?'

Hescroft had looked round the despoiled field. 'You've still got to write a report. Have them dig two trenches out at right angles from that hole. Just to make sure there's really nothing left.'

The new trenches had turned up three tessera fragments and a quarter of a roof tile. It didn't amount to a lot. The only solid evidence they had of what had been there before was a single photo taken by CD of Maxwell's original hole. Morale had been so low by evening that there was little doubt, when it had started to drizzle, that the pub was the right place to go.

The Stag, halfway along the green, was a basic pub with lino on the floor and bright neon lights. Soon after the team had ordered their beers, there was a lot of background giggling going on at their expense. Whatever it was that made it not Friday clearly had something to do with them.

'What do we do now, Patrick?' asked Aidan.

'We finish those two trenches, then I guess—'

Suddenly the reason it wasn't Friday became clear with a loud guitar chord.

'Gawd Almighty,' said Dozer. 'Take a look at Eric Clapton over there.'

The man sitting on the guitar stool wore a cowboy hat and a bright red waistcoat. He strummed another chord or two then launched straight into a song, a simple variation on basic country-and-western hoe-down.

'They came up here to Wytchlow with their trowels all prepared,
To search for Roman ruins that the centuries might have spared.
They dug around all afternoon till it came on to pour
But they didn't like to get too wet so they all packed up at four.
A nice man offered shelter in a barn a mile away
And they slept there like a pile of logs until dawn of the next day.
When they went back to start again, they got a great big shock
Because while they'd all been sleeping, the digger ran amok.
They'd found the Roman pavement, but they didn't think too quick,
'Cos someone came there in the night and played a dirty trick.
When they saw what happened, they could not believe their eyes,
Next time they meet our Roger, they'll be a little *more wise.'*

The crowd roared its approval and the old man in the cloth cap reappeared to make sure Patrick had got the point. '"A *little* more wise", do you get it? Roger Little, eh?'

Patrick nodded wearily, realised that the whole bar was grinning in their direction, and waved in sheepish acknowledgment.

The door opened and Bobby walked in. It was safer to look away, but as she walked across the room she dragged his treacherous gaze after her. She was still wearing her working clothes and that old woollen hat. There was a chorus of greeting.

'How's the great struggle?' called a man in a Barbour jacket.

'We'll win,' she said.

'Bloody right,' said someone else.

'Always done it, always will,' said an old man with brown teeth.

For a few moments Patrick was distracted from the knowledge that was slowly forming in his head, the knowledge that he'd seen the singer before. If you took away the absurd hat and waistcoat, you had the middle-aged man who had been watching them from his position up on the hill. It wasn't only Little who had known what part of the field to dig up. This man had also been watching yesterday as Patrick had paced out the field and Roger Little had laid his destructive plans.

He sought another glimpse of Bobby in the now-crowded bar but all he could see was the top of her hat.

As if he'd read Patrick's mind, Dozer said, 'Do you think she always wears that hat?'

'Scalp condition,' said CD. 'I had a girl once, she had a scalp condition all over. Had to wear a chemical warfare suit. Never did find out what she looked like.'

Bobby was down there at the far end, near the singer, who drained his glass and picked up his guitar again. The bar fell silent once more at the first sound of his fingers on the strings. This was a different sound, a gentle, skilful arpeggio contrasting greatly with the crude strumming of the first song.

'I sing you the song of the German Queen
With her hair dark red and her eyes so green.
I sing you the song of the way they cried
On the dreadful day when the fair queen died.

The eldest child of her father's line,
A slender shoot from a sturdy vine,
She kept his house from her early days
Once her well-loved mother had passed away.'

The pub audience listened in reverential silence but Patrick detected that they were a little puzzled. It seemed to him that the first rough song was more what they were used to than this quiet ballad.

'Her father wore the silver ring
From the German lands where he'd been a king
And, dreaming of what once had been,
He called the girl his German Queen.

There came a time in that gentle land
When their peace was marred by a roving band.
New arrived from the Saxon shore
With a grudge from home and an old, old score.

They climbed the hill on an autumn morn,
And the first light gleamed on the swords they'd drawn.
High on the hill, that glint was seen
By the chieftain's girl with her eyes so green.

She ran to the wall with the warning gong
And she made it sing its arousing song.
Her brothers leapt from their wives' warm arms
At the first loud cry of its harsh alarm.

They met the raiders, blade to blade
In a spray of blood by the old stockade.
Outnumbered by them five to one,
The fight was led by the oldest son.

At the moment when they saw him fall
And his soul took flight to the warriors' hall
The hills rang out to a chilling cry.
Their father saw the young prince die.'

Patrick slipped into a reverie, flashing back to the first time he'd ever been on a big stage, to the awesome, terrifying, thrilling moment of walking into a bombardment of howling applause. Rachel, worried, watching in the wings. Pat taking the first step towards being Paddy, tilted off-balance by the first taste of massive, uncritical adulation. He saw Rachel clearly in his mind's eye then, but it wasn't his mind's eye at all because this version of her was standing at the bar looking at the singer. Patrick stared at Bobby for an age, then she met his eye and frowned at the intensity of his gaze.

He blinked and broke the eye contact, and, as he became aware that he'd lost the thread of the song, he saw that the singer had got up and was coming towards him and his diggers, directing his song straight at them.

'Up on the hill on the sacred ground,
They dug a grave in the ancient mound.
They laid her there and in sorrow kneeled
Round that older tomb in the Bury Field.

Amber beads were round her head
And she sleeps there still on her wooden bed.
Her cloak secured with the royal jewel
That had marked the years of her father's rule.

Now leather and wood have turned to dust.
The iron brackets are dark brown rust.
The bed has lost its strength and weight
But the burden on it's no longer great.

The years and the plough have flattened the land
Which she saved with a stroke of her valiant hand.
Now silence and shadows mark the scene
Of the glorious grave of the German Queen.'

He bowed his head to the applause and Patrick was left utterly astonished at what he had just heard. A crude folk song, describing in detail something almost unknown except in the academic realms of archaeology—an Anglo-Saxon furnished bed burial. Was it just chance? What had he missed in the rest of the song?

Patrick looked across the table at the American. 'What did you make of that?'

'The chicken sword? Funny you should ask . . .'

'Chicken sword? What's a chicken sword? I meant the bed burial.'

'Well, I don't know much about—'

'Hang on. He's going. I've got to talk to him.'

The singer was making for the door. It took Patrick a moment or two to push through the crowd after him and, by the time he got out, the man was just a dark shape moving across the village green.

'Wait a minute,' called Patrick. 'Can I talk to you?'

The man didn't slow down and Patrick ran after him to catch up.

'I just want to know about that song you sang,' he said.

No response.

'I only want to know what it's called? Who wrote it?'

The man looked round at him and strode onwards.

'What's going on?' said Patrick angrily, trying to keep up. 'Why won't you talk to me? Was it you who dug up our field?'

At that the man swung round, made an emphatic gesture of rejection in complete silence, and pushed Patrick in the chest.

'Don't you bloody do that,' said Patrick, and grabbed the offending arm only to have his own arm seized from behind and wrenched away. He swung round to find himself confronting Bobby.

'Go home, Joe,' she told the singer. 'Go home. I'll sort him out.'

The man looked at her, grunted and walked off.

'That's Joe?' said Patrick, aghast. 'Your Joe?'

'Yes, that's Joe. What the bloody *hell* did you think you were doing, treating him like that?'

The anger in Bobby's voice was more than he could deal with. Now she didn't just look like Rachel, she sounded like her too.

'I didn't know that was Joe. I was only trying to talk to him.'

'You weren't. I saw you. You were pushing and grabbing at him.'

'I thought he was being pretty rude. He wouldn't answer.'

She laughed derisively. 'He *couldn't* answer, for God's sake. He doesn't talk. Don't say nobody in the pub told you!'

That made no sense. 'Come off it. I've just heard him singing.'

'Yes, he sings. He doesn't talk apart from that, can't get any words out. Even to me. He hasn't talked for years. There's no reason to go bullying him like that.' She was calming down a little.

'Bobby, I had no idea.' It was the first time he had said her name. He had to do it, to establish for himself who she was. 'I didn't know any of that. I wouldn't have gone chasing after him if they'd told me. Why is he like that?'

She made a noise of exasperation, the sound of someone who had been asked that question far too many times. 'I don't know. He talked when he was little then he just stopped.'

'And he doesn't talk to you, either?'

'He writes me notes.'

'I don't understand about the singing. How can he do that?'

'That's his way. He puts on his clothes and he's someone else. He's a performer, he's not Joe any more. Maybe he just needs to be somebody else. I know I should be able to explain it, but I can't. It's pretty hard to understand.'

'No it's not,' said Patrick, thinking just how much he knew about the lure of being somebody else on a big stage with the world looking on. In the dark, he could just see the shine of her wide eyes, turned on him. A door opened and closed somewhere behind him and the light from it showed him her face, framed in dark hair, the hat gone, and she was not Rachel because Rachel was blonde.

'I heard,' she said, 'that you used to sing.'

'Who have you been talking to? CD? Dozer?' Without wishing it, there was a harsh edge in his voice.

'No, no. It was one of the diggers, the guy with the round glasses.'

'Aidan?' Jesus. Did everybody know?

'Listen, Patrick, I didn't mean to upset you. It's none of my business.'

They were both silent as the echoes of discord died away.

'That song he was singing,' said Patrick, driven by the need to say something as well as by the need to know, '"The German Queen" and all that. Do you know it?'

'I've heard bits of it,' she said.

'Do you know where it comes from?'

'I think Dad taught it to him. Joe used to have a terrible stutter. Dad taught him old songs to help him talk but then, after Dad died, he stopped talking completely.'

'You and Joe were brought up together?'

'Of course we were.' He could see the pale disc of her face tilt as she put it on one side. 'He's my brother. Didn't you know that either?'

A younger sister protecting her damaged older brother. It began to make sense. She hadn't seemed like half of a couple.

'No, I didn't . . . Do you think he'll sing it again? In the pub?'

'I don't think so. He usually sings his own stuff. It's how he manages, see? All week he saves up all the things he wants to say and he makes them into songs. Just once in a while, when he's had his say, he'll sing one of Dad's old songs. You can't really ask him to do it. He's not very biddable, Joe. He sticks to his routines.'

'He didn't tonight. It's not Friday.'

'He sang tonight because of what's happened, because of you.'

'He was poking fun at us.'

'That was just his way. It wouldn't do to take your side openly against a villager. Think about it. His real message was that Little did it and that's what people will remember. Did you mind?'

'Yes.'

'I think he realised that. I think he sang the other song as a sort of present, to make up for it.'

'So it wasn't Joe who dug up the field?'

'Joe? Why on earth did you think it was Joe?'

'He was up there watching. I paced out the area we'd surveyed, the same bit that got dug up. Little was there, but Joe saw it too.'

'Listen to me. Joe would sooner cut his own arm off than damage anything from the past. He was beside himself when he heard what Little had done.'

'OK. I understand. Thank you for explaining. By the way, what was all that other stuff about? The business at the school?'

'Oh, that. I'll tell you sometime.'

'There might not be a sometime. We'll pack up soon, I expect.'

'Really? Damn. I've been looking forward to this dig.'

'We'll see how it goes tomorrow. Time I went back.' And because it was so very dark, Patrick added, 'Shall I see you home first?' and was discomfited when she burst out laughing.

She cut her laugh off with a hand over her mouth. 'I'm sorry. I didn't mean to be rude.'

The night hid his flush. 'I just meant it's very dark.'

'Yes, I know. I've lived here an awfully long time. I've managed all right so far.' Then, as if to take the sting out of her words, she went on, 'All the newcomers who move here start asking for streetlamps. We've managed to fight them off so far. One night, they look up and notice all the stars and after that it's all right. They get the point.'

He watched her as she strode away, then groped his way back to the field and crawled into his tent. Lying in his clammy sleeping-bag feeling miserable, he heard the diggers coming back from the pub, the diggers who, it seemed, all knew about Paddy Kane.

There was much to-ing and fro-ing and then a flickering glow through the walls of the tent as branches were fed into crackling flames. Next came unwelcome footsteps, close to his tent.

'Patrick, old bean. Are you awake?'

He pretended not to hear, but CD just cranked up the volume. 'Patrick. Yoohoo, Patrick.'

'What?'

'Are you awake?'

'I am now.'

'Come and join in the fun.'

'Not tonight, I'm tired.'

'Don't be a party-pooper. Guess what I've got in my pocket.'

'I don't know,' said Patrick wearily, who also didn't really care.

'Just a bottle of Glenboggy eight-hundred-year-old malt.'

'No, it's OK. Enjoy yourselves. I'm tired.'

'Hey, listen up. It's kind of like our last night. They'd like to see you. Gaye's got made up specially.'

'What?'

'Yeah, she got pissed and fell in the mud. Face first. She thinks it's funny. Hey, listen, Patrick, *I'd* like to see you. Come on out of there.'

So, reluctantly, Patrick joined the diggers round the fire.

'What did you want that singer bloke for, Pat?' asked Dozer. 'Saw you chase out after him.'

'That song. It was just something I wanted to know. But he's not a talker,' said Patrick.

'Yeah. They gave us the form in the pub,' said CD. 'Weird, eh? After he'd finished that song you said something about a bed.'

'Well, yes. I just had an idea that the song was about a bed burial.'

'Listen, my period's the Romans, not all this Saxon shit. You know the way it is on an Anglo-Saxon dig. You get really excited when the dirt changes colour 'cos maybe you've hit a hole. It's just like the song—silence and shadows. Give me something you can bounce a trowel off any day.'

'Hang on. Yesterday you said you hated all that Roman stuff.'

'That was yesterday. Whatever I'm doing, I like the opposite best.'

'You don't know about bed burials?' asked Patrick, feeling pleased that there was at least one area where he knew as much as the American. 'Have you read the Swallowcliffe report?'

'Nope. What's the gist?' CD passed Patrick the bottle.

He tried a small swig. A corrosive liquid seared his throat and kicked his brain from underneath. 'Jesus, what's that?' he said.

'You've not tried Glenboggy before?' said CD. 'Well, as they say in the traditional distilleries of the South Bronx, there's always a first time but there's not often a second time. You were saying?'

'I've got this thing about place names,' said Patrick, 'so I like this story. This guy Speake went back over the notes for a dig someone did years ago and never published. He put it all together from the finds and the dig notebook. Everything had been stacked away in dusty old boxes for heaven knows how long. It was a Bronze Age barrow down south of Stonehenge and in it they found an Anglo-Saxon woman, surrounded by all kinds of iron brackets. They realised she had been buried on a bed and they managed to work out what it had looked like. The way the song described it, the leather straps and stuff, that was pretty much the way it was.'

'So what's the business with the place names?'

'On the old charters, this burial mound was always called Posses Low. So everyone thought that someone called Poss had been buried there. Thing is, in among the finds were all kinds of bits of gold and silver and bronze, and when they put them together they realised they made up a really elaborate shoulder bag, a satchel. A pretty distinctive piece of kit. That's when they realised that *pusa* is the Old English for a bag and Posses Low might have literally meant the grave of the bag lady.'

'Nice,' said Dozer. 'Low as in Wytchlow.'

Patrick became aware that a silence had fallen and people were shuffling up towards their end of the circle to listen.

'What would the "Wytch" bit be?' someone said.

'Maybe a personal name.'

'You have to beware of creating a false tradition from the name of a place,' said Peter Knight. 'For people who couldn't read and write it was a bit tempting sometimes. They kept doing it in the *Anglo-Saxon Chronicle*, you know. They invented this man Port and his sons who landed at Portsmouth, when the name came from the Latin *portus*.'

'Well, anyway,' said Patrick lamely, 'it sounded to me like the song was about a real burial. But I expect it was all just chance.'

'I don't think so,' said CD. 'It wasn't just the bed, was it? There was the sword too. Could be there's an archaeologist out there writing songs. A whole new style, archo-rock.'

'I dig it,' said Dozer to a chorus of groans.

'I didn't hear the bit about the sword,' said Patrick. 'What was it?

Aidan, sitting in the lotus position straight on the wet grass with his round glasses reflecting flames, spoke in a lilting voice. '"The robber band, they turned and ran, before the wrath of a righteous man, leaving their dead where . . ." What was it now? ". . . where they'd been laid by the slashing edge of that chicken blade."'

'Hey, that's pretty impressive,' said CD. 'Can you do the rest of it?'

'That verse just stuck,' said Aidan.

'So what's this chicken blade, then?' said Dozer.

'You better all have some more Glenboggy,' said CD. 'The tale I am about to tell makes shaggy dogs look clean-shaven. It is *decidedly* far-fetched and there's nothing like Glenboggy to dull the critical faculties. I make it myself specifically for that purpose.'

'I bet it's not as far-fetched as that time you an' I got stuck in the Aztec tomb with the bats,' said Dozer.

'It comes close,' said CD, 'pretty close.' He looked at Patrick, owlish behind his pebble glasses. 'OK, here goes. Now it just happens that the first thesis I ever wrote for my doctorate was all about the evidence concerning sword manufacture in the Old Norse myths.'

All the diggers had squeezed in close to the fire, to hear better. Stifled chokes betrayed the course of CD's bottle.

'There's an Old Norse myth called Thiorik's Saga,' CD told them. 'It's the first detailed description of how they made old swords. A good smith would pick the right iron and twist bars of different grades together, so that when they were heated and hammered in the forging you'd get a really good blade. If a bad smith screwed up, the blade would bend halfway through a fight. Not good news for the guy holding the handle. Well, in the saga, there's this smith called Velent or Weland or Wayland, who promises to make his lord a really strong sword. So he makes this sword called Mimming, and when he finishes it he starts filing away at it. Nothing odd in that. Only thing is, Velent went right on filing until the blade was just a pile of shiny filings on the floor. He sweeps it up and mixes it with grain, OK? After that, he starves his chickens for three days and then he feeds them the mixture of filings and corn. Then guess what he does next.'

'Roasts them,' said Dozer.

'He collects their droppings. He collects the chicken shit, guys and gals, and he shapes it into a blade and he forges it all over again and there he has it, a nice shiny, hard sword. But he doesn't stop there. Oh no, you don't get into sagas by doing things the easy way. He did it *three times*. In the end, Velent has this amazing blade that's much smaller and as strong as hell, which he inlays with gold ready to give to his boss man.'

'Who goes out and kills lots of people with it?' suggested Maxwell.

'No, that would be just a little bit simple for your average Norse saga. What he then does is he makes an exact replica of the sword out of really crap metal and he gives *that* one to the king.'

'So what happened next?'

'No idea. I lost interest about there. I guess the king got killed and his kids sued Velent under the Sale of Goods Act.'

Aidan was in questioning mood. 'It's got to be a load of rubbish, right? I mean, you couldn't actually *make* a sword that way?'

'*Au contraire*,' said CD. 'What does chicken shit smell of? Ammonia. That's because it's full of nitrogen, and when you forge iron with nitrogen you get nitrides and that is just exactly what you want for a good strong blade.'

'So the chicken blade could be true?' said Dozer.

'Could be,' said CD.

FOUR

Patrick woke abruptly at just past six in the morning, when the tent collapsed on him, to find himself smothered in damp polyester and horizontal tent poles. He struggled out of his sleeping-bag, and slithered out onto wet grass. His heart was racing because he knew it was impossible that his tent could collapse so suddenly and comprehensively without the intervention of some outside agency. These igloo-type tents didn't come apart easily.

He got out expecting to see a stray cow standing there, but there was no visible explanation. The rest of the campsite was silent and in good order. Perplexed, Patrick bent down to wrestle the poles back into place. There was a noise from behind him like stone striking stone, and only then did he look round, up at the hill behind their field, where Joe was now standing just the other side of the fence.

Patrick stared at him, frightened by the knowledge that Joe must have come to his tent and pulled his tent poles apart. Was this a punishment for his own aggression last night? He stared across at the older man. Then Joe lifted a hand in a summoning gesture.

Dressed only in the long T-shirt he'd slept in, Patrick found himself raising a hand in acknowledgment and pointing at his tent as if to explain he needed clothes. He groped inside for jeans, socks and boots, pulled them on and looked up to find that Joe was now well on his way up the hill.

Patrick wriggled through the fence, and the field beyond was rough pasture with tussocks of grass that tricked his feet as he climbed the gentle slope, so that he was forced to look down. But whenever he looked up again, he saw Joe standing waiting for him.

The rise of the hill was deceptive and the undulating shape of the land didn't reveal itself until Patrick had got to where he'd last seen Joe. He was on a gently domed plateau with fields and woodland to the west and the land falling away towards Oxford to the southeast. Joe stood a hundred yards away, facing him, stock-still, and when he was sure Patrick was looking at him, he pointed emphatically at the earth by his feet, then walked rapidly away.

Patrick fixed the spot with his eyes and, when Joe had disappeared out of sight into a copse of trees, walked slowly towards it. There was nothing remarkable to see, so he crouched and ran his fingers through the short grass. He had no idea what he was looking for.

Moving thirty paces to one side of the spot, he got down on the ground and did four slow press-ups, his head raised, staring at the place Joe had indicated. It was an old trick, shown to him on his very first student dig. The change in perspective as he lifted himself up and down, just a foot off the ground, gave him an exaggerated view of the small changes in the topography of the land ahead.

He suddenly knew what Joe had been pointing at. The very top of the hill rose just a fraction more steeply than the natural curve of the land, making a flattened dome maybe fifteen yards across. The evidence was slender, but after he'd looked carefully at it for several minutes he was convinced he was looking at a barrow, a Bronze Age burial mound, flattened by the slow erosion of wind and rain.

Patrick felt a sudden disappointment. A Bronze Age barrow was interesting enough. It did not square, however, with Anglo-Saxon bed burials. There had been an absurd hope at the back of his mind that Joe's song had meant that at the end of this mysterious journey there might be a clue to the last resting place of his German Queen. Instead there was something that predated it by over a thousand years.

He sat down on the ground on the top of the flattened barrow mound, wondering again why Joe had brought him to this spot. It was the first moment he'd had for reflection since this doomed dig began, and reflection wasn't something Patrick enjoyed. In the years since he had reformed his life, reflection had taken the shape of self-accusation more than anything else. But in the past two days, something had changed. He put it down to the fact that, despite himself, he was enjoying the company of these people: CD's nonchalant wit, Dozer's solidity, even Aidan and Maxwell. The truth was that he had started to become a real person again and the process was painful. For a moment his mind brought Bobby into the equation but Bobby was a dangerous diversion; Bobby took him back to a Rachel he still loved and couldn't blame for what had happened to David.

David would have run down this hillside. David, his dark, liquid hair flying behind him, would have jumped on his stocky legs and fallen over without minding, and rummaged in the earth for sticks and stones to produce as jewels. The earth was always full of treasure for David.

All this time Patrick had been fiddling, running his fingers through the soft soil of the molehill on which his right hand was resting. As his thoughts took this painful turn he toyed with one larger stone in his fingers like a worry bead.

Gradually, its cylindrical regularity forced itself through to the front of his mind and he opened his palm and looked down at it. Many an experienced eye has been misled by a freakishly regular piece of natural stone, but not many stones are shaped like cylinders with a tubular hole running through them. Patrick spat in his palm, rubbed the surface with his finger, and colour, bright yellow man-made colour, burst through its coating of grey soil dust. It was opaque yellow glass, decorated with thin red lines in a characteristic crossing-wave pattern, finely worked, beautiful—and datable.

Anglo-Saxon. Seventh century. He'd drawn Saxon beads by the hundred in his recent catching-up studies. This one was perfect—a bead you might easily find in a seventh-century burial. Joe's song had said something about beads, amber beads around her head. This wasn't amber but it did well as a substitute.

Patrick sat looking at the bead in his hand, not as an artefact heading for a glass case, but as a messenger, bursting out of the earth with a tale to tell.

He looked down the hill towards Wytchlow. 'Low' often meant a burial mound, 'low' from the old Saxon *hlaew*. Dozer had said last night that 'Wytch' could be a personal name, so this could be Wytch's low, the place where Wytch was buried. But there was the great forest of Wychwood too. The wood of the Hwicca? The double 'c' of Hwicca has a 'ch' sound. Something else was nagging at him, something he had read. It wouldn't come back.

The Hwicca were a mongrel race, without simple roots. Saxons from the north German coast and Angles from the southern Danish peninsula, they had been pushed out by rising sea levels in front and rising population behind, taking to their boats for a fresh start. What had they made of this alien landscape? He looked down towards the ruined field. The remains of Roman buildings would still have been a dominant presence, left behind as those who had organised Roman Britain fled for home. The Angles and the Saxons didn't use stone. They used up their creative energy more often in their possessions than in their housing. Post-holes for their houses, most of them little more than timber tents, were the only lasting evidence of their construction efforts. What could they have thought of the Romans' almost magical constructions? Civilisation crumbled fast in the 200 years between the Romans' departure and the burial of this bead. Four hundred years of occupation had taught the Britons how to enjoy the Roman way of life but not how to maintain it when the teachers had left.

Patrick knew that British and English were not synonyms then, far from it. English meant Angles, the Germanic incomers. British meant Britons, the Celtic people who'd been here long before the Romans came. The incoming 'English' and their neighbours the Saxons displaced the British by some unknown mixture of violence and integration. Archaeology showed, most fascinatingly of all, that quite suddenly, after AD 600, Anglo-Saxon attitudes changed. They began to annex the old Roman sites that they'd skirted for 150 years with new confidence, using the ruins as burial places for the most important among their dead. At the same time, they began to use much more ancient earthworks too, inserting their dead, cuckoo-like, into these old nests.

Then, in the middle of his thoughts, he remembered what was nagging him about the possible origin of the name of Wytchlow. Something he'd read, some dissertation on Oxfordshire place names, had suggested an older name for the village: 'Wytchamlow'. Wicham, in its various forms, was a name the Anglo-Saxons started using soon after their arrival, and it generally indicated a place associated with an old Roman site, often just by an old major Roman road.

Wytchamlow, the burial mound by the Roman ruins. It made

sense. And who, he wondered, was the Saxon cuckoo in the old mound on which he was now sitting? Could it possibly be Joe's valiant German Queen on her wooden bed?

PATRICK HAD COME BACK down the hill with a secret in his pocket and a wild idea. He went straight into the catering tent where Bobby was serving solid porridge, and poured himself a mug of tea. She looked startlingly fresh against the frowsy queue of camping-crumpled diggers and she had a smile for everyone. She stared at Patrick curiously. Unsettled, he ran his fingers through his hair.

'Morning,' she said. 'How are you?'

'Good morning,' he answered, smiling. 'I've been up to the top of the hill. That is your field up there, isn't it?'

'Yes,' she said, 'and the field beyond.'

'Do you plough it?'

'No, it's just rough pasture really. There's hardly any soil.' She wondered why he looked so pleased. She had been wondering about him and the diggers' rumours of his past. This seemed a different Patrick who faced her now, a Patrick with someone there behind the eyes, someone who looked straight at you. They said he'd been a legend. Until this morning it had been hard to see how that could be. He looked fully alive for the first time since they'd met.

He left the tent as abruptly as he'd come. Well away from other ears, knowing the odds were stacked against him, he dialled Hescroft on the mobile phone.

'We're wrapping up this afternoon, John.'

'It's a big disappointment, Patrick. I don't need to tell you. All that effort and planning gone for nothing.'

'Well, there is one thing . . .'

'What's that?'

'I think I've found another site.'

'What do you mean?'

'A possible Saxon burial in a barrow just up the hill. Unknown, I'm sure.' He must be mad, he thought, to be inflating the slender evidence. Anyway why should Paradigm Site Check care? It was in it for the money, not for knowledge for its own sake.

There was silence, then a wholly unexpected response. 'Really? Now that's something else. Whose land is it?'

'Bobby's, the woman you hired to cook.'

'And you think it might be the real thing?'

'Well . . . too early to tell. But yes.'

'Would she let us dig?'

Us? 'I'm pretty sure she would.'

'I'll be out in an hour or so.'

Patrick ended the call in a state of pleasant bewilderment, astonished that Hescroft hadn't dismissed his idea out of hand. He was gazing up at the hill in thought when a hesitant voice behind him said, 'Patrick?', and he looked round to see Bobby there.

'Yes?'

'I didn't mean to disturb you. It looked like you were thinking. It's just I wanted to know how many more meals you'll need.'

When she talked, it wasn't so bad. She didn't sound like Rachel.

'I don't know yet,' he said, 'but it might depend on you.'

'How do you mean?'

'Joe led me up the hill this morning. Did you know there's a burial mound at the top, an old barrow? He pointed it out to me.'

'I can't think of anything up there that looks like a barrow.'

'You hardly notice it unless you know where to look. It's there right enough, and what's more, I found something too. Have a look.'

Patrick showed her the yellow glass cylinder and watched with pleasure as she turned it in her fingers, entranced by it.

'It's Anglo-Saxon,' he said, 'much more recent than the barrow. I think there must be a later burial there. I went on looking and found these.' He brought out of his pocket two short grey pieces of what could have been dry wood.

'Bones?' she said, taking one from him. 'Human toe bones.'

'Yes. How do you know?'

'Oh, I know some things. They're pretty distinctive.'

She gave it back. 'So when you say it might depend on me . . .?'

'I'd like to get my boss to agree to let us dig a trial trench up there, while we've got everyone together. You would have to give your agreement. It's your land.'

'Mine and Joe's—not just mine. He'd have to agree too.'

'I think he would. He showed me the place, after all.'

'I'll ask him if it's all right,' she said. 'He'll let me know one way or another if he doesn't agree.'

JOHN HESCROFT CAME into the field, not in his own car but as the passenger in a huge black Toyota Land Cruiser with metallic red logos on the doors. Patrick read the words 'Belwether Productions, Film and TV', and began, belatedly, to smell a rat.

Hescroft had a wide public-relations smile on his face. 'Want you to meet Kenny, Patrick. Kenny Camden from Belwether. Kenny, this is our new young superstar, Patrick Kane.'

And what did Kenny Camden say, smiling a tobacco-stained smile, long white hair flowing in the wind, but, 'Hi, Paddy. It's a great pleasure to meet you.'

'It's Patrick.'

Kenny gave a conspiratorial wink. 'OK. Patrick. Got it.'

'What about this new site?' said Hescroft. 'Give us the lowdown.'

'New site?' said CD, walking up. 'Hi, John.' Then he stuck his hand out to the TV producer. 'Hi, I'm CD, Mr C. D. Corcoran, if you want to be formal.'

'Kenny Camden. I read your piece on the Ridgeway hill-forts.'

'Wow, that makes three—you, me and my mother.'

'No, no, I was impressed,' said Camden smoothly. 'What do you think of this burial mound of Patrick's?'

Patrick saw that this was the point at which everything would fall to pieces. He hadn't even shown CD the bead.

'Too early to tell,' said CD, 'but you never know, do you? Better let Patrick talk you through it. I'll just listen. I'd love to hear it all over again.' He turned a beaming smile on Patrick, who blessed him from the bottom of his heart.

'There's a burial site at the top of this hill, an Anglo-Saxon burial inserted in an older barrow with a ring-ditch round it, possibly Bronze Age,' said Patrick, picking his words carefully. 'I was shown the place early this morning by someone who's lived here a long time. I found this in the soil.' He brought out the bead.

Hescroft whistled. 'Look at that! Typically Anglo-Saxon.'

'Ain't she a little beauty?' said CD, as if he had seen the bead before.

'Then there are these,' Patrick said, showing them the bones.

'Human,' said CD after the briefest of glances, 'definitely human.'

Hescroft and the producer exchanged significant looks.

'Well, now,' said Hescroft, 'Kenny wants to shoot a pilot to see if he can get one of the major TV companies interested in a series. We were going to suggest shooting the Roman dig until . . .'

'This is better,' said Kenny. 'We'll be in from the start.'

'There might be nothing there,' said Patrick faintly.

Kenny shrugged. 'It's only a couple of days' shooting to find out. It'll make a great show. I can see it now. The wild man of rock puts down his guitar and picks up a trowel.'

'What did you say?' Patrick swung round on Hescroft. 'What have you been telling him?'

'Nothing,' said Hescroft, astonished.

'Leave it out, Paddy,' said Kenny. 'He didn't tell me. He didn't have to. You've got a short memory. I shot your second video, remember?'

Of course he didn't. You just hired people to do things like that. They weren't people you noticed.

'OK,' said Camden, 'you've lost the hair but you're not hard to spot. You did the greatest disappearing act since Elvis. Everybody wants to know what happened to Paddy Kane and Nam Erewhon.'

'Nam what?' said Hescroft.

'Erewhon as in Samuel Butler's Utopian ideal, but more appropriately "Nowhere Man" backwards. They were the antidote to the Beatles. You really don't know who you've got here?' Kenny looked at Hescroft in surprise. The man who wrote "Wedding Vows". The man who—'

'That's my business,' interrupted Patrick. 'I don't want all that brought up. I just want to forget it, OK?'

'Not OK, no,' said Kenny. 'This show stands or falls on human interest, on you being in it. You haven't changed that much, chum. People are still going to notice you even if we don't tell them.'

'No way,' said Patrick. 'Absolutely no way.'

'John,' said the producer, 'let's you and I sit in the car and talk this through. Then we'll have a little talk with your boy here.'

Patrick stalked back down the field with CD.

The American cast around for something to say. 'Listen, it doesn't matter. He's just a TV tosser.'

Silence.

'Patrick, what difference does it make? Everybody here knows you used to be famous.'

'How do they know that? Because you told them?'

'No way. One of the other guys recognised you. Old Doze and I, we did our best. We . . .'

'You mean you two have been going around talking about me?'

'Hey, now that's enough, mister. Yeah, we did. We went around asking people to lay off you. Do you have a problem with that?'

'Yes. I'm not a freak show. I'm not there for people to tiptoe round me, gossiping when I can't hear.'

'The jury's out on that one. You're behaving like some kind of freak show.'

Patrick swung round on him, furious, then saw CD's eyes had nothing but concern in them.

He exhaled noisily. 'I'm sorry. Maybe I've got this a little out of perspective.'

'That's OK. Look, I don't know what you've been through but if you want to talk about it . . .'

Patrick had constructed his recent life around not talking about his past. The offer was kind but it hurt.

'CD, I know you mean well but there is nothing, absolutely nothing in my old life I want to talk about. I wish none of it had happened. I would dearly like it to be'—he was about to say 'buried' but the image of the graves in the Welsh churchyard punched him in the stomach—'forgotten.'

SITTING IN THE LAND CRUISER, Kenny Camden was spelling it out to John Hescroft. 'Now listen, John, you've got to talk to the boy. Make him understand. He knows about publicity.'

'What do I say to him? You heard him.'

'You say to him: you want to dig this barrow—you front the

show. That's the price you pay, take it or leave it.'

'You mean you make it clear he was this . . . this rock star.'

The producer considered and grinned. 'You don't have to spell that out. Tell him we'll let him just be Patrick Kane, archaeologist.' The hell we will, he thought. This one is going to leak and then just watch the viewing figures.

SO IN THE END Patrick, though he knew he was supping with the devil, had little choice. The song and the bead had got him and he could not leave the mound alone. The only way they could dig on the hill was if Kenny Camden would pay some of the bills.

When supper had been served in the catering tent, Patrick caught Bobby in the middle of clearing up and said, 'I need to talk to you about the barrow. When will you see Joe?'

'As soon as I get this lot back.' She indicated the stack of dirty pans. 'I'll come back over and tell you his reaction if you like. Probably not until about nine thirty.'

When she'd gone, Patrick called everybody together.

'You know this dig's over,' he told them, 'and I'm very sorry about the circumstances. Some of you, I know, are disappointed not to get the chance to do a proper dig. Well, I don't want to raise your hopes too much but there's a possibility we could go straight on to another dig very close to here. I won't be able to tell you much more until tomorrow morning but think about it.'

He was about to let them go, then, on the spur of the moment, he decided there was after all something more to say. 'Also . . . I know that some of you have picked up the fact that I used to be, um . . . well, involved in the music business.' It would have been good to make some sort of joke out of it, but humour was unknown in the mental Siberia that made up this part of his life. 'That's something I've left behind, so please, if you don't mind, allow me just to be an archaeologist for the purposes of this dig.'

They all seemed to be looking at him very hard. Aidan nodded slowly and Gaye looked round at her neighbours with a disconcertingly conspiratorial expression on her face.

They all went to the pub but Patrick found it easy to resist their invitations to go too. He suspected that they needed a break without him, to discuss him in all probability, and he found he didn't really care what they said.

There were nearly two hours to kill before meeting Bobby, so he walked down the lane into the centre of the village. At the far end there was a village hall with lights on inside it. He stopped and looked in. Two women were on their knees in the middle of the floor, painting an old cart a glossy black. It had two wheels at the back, a smaller one at the front and a long wooden handle to tow it along. Inside was a seat of cracked and desiccated leather. A Victorian Bath chair, he thought.

Patrick was inspecting this strange vehicle, when a hand grabbed at his legs. He looked down in shock to see a small devil tugging at his knees, cackling. It was half his height but its face was no child's. It was dark and deformed, covered in disturbing, crawling shapes.

'No, stop that,' he said, alarmed. 'Leave me alone.'

A woman's voice from inside the hall yelled, 'Mikey!' and the creature rushed out of sight round the corner.

Patrick took a deep breath and walked away, heading back to the camp, wondering just what he had seen.

Back at the marquee, he dragged one of the catering tables outside, set up a folding chair and lit a candle inside a jam jar.

He tried to draw the Anglo-Saxon bead on which his entire burial theory rested and, as he dragged the jam jar closer to light his sketchpad, the flame flared, sending a brief splash of red, green and blue light out through the jar's lurid label and across the white sheet of paper. Immediately, with a flood of pain, he was back in Italy.

In Perugia Cathedral, in limbo between his betrayal and the retribution that immediately followed, he had watched a small boy playing on the solemn floor, entranced by the spangles of colour dashed across the stone by the Italian sun through the stained glass. The memory of that boy conjured David out of the darkness just as it had at the time. David, brimming with trust and love and promise.

When Bobby came quietly back to the field, she saw in the candlelight that Patrick's cheeks were wet. Staring at his face, she wasn't sure if he knew she was there. She waited until his head moved fractionally towards her, then spoke softly. 'Hello, Patrick?

I just came to tell you that I told Joe what you said and he did a little dance.'

There was more silence, because Patrick was dragging himself back from where he'd been and didn't yet trust himself to speak.

'You can start when you like,' she said to fill the gap. 'I suppose you'll have to move all the tents out of here but there's a good flat space at the top of the hill. I can move stuff with the tractor and trailer if it would help. I'm sure we could manage if everyone—'

'"How beautifully blue the sky, the glass is rising very high. Continue fine I hope it may, and yet it rained but yesterday",' said Patrick.

'I think I'm missing something here,' she said cautiously.

His voice sounded normal to him now. 'Gilbert and Sullivan,' he said. 'It's a song the chorus sings to fill up an embarrassing silence. Is it *The Pirates of Penzance*? I can't remember.'

'You could ask Peter. He'd probably know. Was that what I was doing? Filling an embarrassing silence?'

'Weren't you?'

'I wasn't embarrassed. I just thought you needed a moment or two.'

'Yeah, I did. Thanks. Would you like a glass of wine?'

And so they sat there on opposite sides of a flimsy wooden table and the low yellow light lit one side of Bobby's face in a new and startling way so that Patrick saw just ivory curves and deep shadows. Her hair was tied back, dark in the candlelight, banishing Rachel.

He looked for safe ground. 'I saw something odd in the village. They were painting this old cart.'

'Ah. That's not just an old cart. That's the May Queen's carriage. It's May Day in nine days.'

'What happens on May Day?'

He knew at once that this might be safe ground for him but it wasn't for her. There was a note of bitterness in her voice when she replied. 'Normally something lovely. This year, maybe a revolution.' She sighed. 'There's a row going on in the village. It may sound a bit trivial to an outsider but it's one of those really divisive things.'

'Tell me.'

'There's a tradition here going back heaven knows how long. Everyone gets up at dawn on May Morning and we all go out into the meadow down by the river and pick the flowers while the dew is still on them. The children put the dew in little bottles for their mothers because if you put May Morning dew on your face, you lose your wrinkles. Did you know that?'

'I didn't.'

'After that, there's a big breakfast. Then we all decorate the cart with flowers and we push the May Queen round the village in it before the Maypole dancing.'

'So why the revolution?'

'There's a new head teacher and he's really into tests and league tables and all that. He says the May Day traditions have got to happen at the weekend this year, out of school time, because the National Curriculum doesn't leave any room for it. I mean to say, what harm would a couple of hours do? He must be mad.'

'Isn't there anybody else you can go to? What about the school governors?'

She shook her head. 'They're on his side. It's a Church of England primary school and we had a great vicar up to last year, but he's gone and now this awful old man has come in. He's straight out of Anthony Trollope, extraordinarily narrow-minded. He says it's a pagan festival and it's unchristian to celebrate it.'

'I suppose technically he's got a point.'

'Oh yes? Christmas was a pagan festival if you want to be purist. But really, what does that matter compared to the fact that this has been happening year in year out for as long as anyone can remember? There are old ladies of eighty who remember when they were May Queen. You should see their faces when the cart comes past their doors . . .' Her voice trailed off for a moment. 'Do you know why he really hates it? Because there's a lovely old carving that they put on the front of the cart. It's a sort of wooden mask with lots of little holes in. They push the stalks of the flowers into the holes so it comes to life. It's a face with two birds flying out of the mouth and a sort of beard made of leaves and fruits.'

'I've seen it,' said Patrick, remembering the little demon tugging at his knees. 'Is it a Green Man?'

'That's what the vicar says. He says it's pagan. Well, you get Green Man carvings in churches all over the place. He's just got some real beef against anything that's fun. I can't stand him.'

'What about the other school governors?'

'Guess who's the chairman?'

'I don't really know anyone round here except . . . Ah. Roger Little?'

'Precisely. He's only lived here three years. The vicar says it's good to have a businessman as chairman. I ask you.'

'So what are you going to do?'

'Mass disobedience. Most of the parents are on my side. They're going to take their kids out of school that morning and do it anyway. The head teacher says he'll suspend any child for a week who's not in school that day. It's absurd.'

'So that's what was happening when I nearly ran you over? But why are you so involved in this? Have you got children in the school?'

'Oh God. No, of course I haven't. I *was* a child. I did that procession every year I was in the school. I think it really matters. That bloody man's got no sense of the history of it.'

'Would it really make a difference if you did it a couple of days later?'

'Would you mind having Christmas the following Thursday?'

'I wouldn't really care,' he said.

'You haven't got kids?'

He breathed out sharply and his throat closed up on his words. He just shook his head.

She moved her head slightly to one side. Now the light spilled into her eyes and, dismayingly, the distancing hair lost in the darkness, she was the young Rachel looking at him again, concerned and close.

'I only know a bit about your band and your songs but you don't strike me as the sort of person who would do anything terrible. Why are you so harsh on yourself? What is this enormous price you've decided you have to pay?'

He tried to deflect her. 'You don't know I'm harsh on myself.'

'I have eyes and ears. I've rarely seen someone suffering as much as you are, Patrick. You've got a hair shirt on every second of the day. You jump down the throat of people who want to help you. It's like you're burning yourself to death from the inside. You can tell me to leave you alone but you can't tell me you're not suffering.'

He turned sharply to one side so that he didn't have to look at her. 'If I am, I deserve it.'

'What did you do to deserve it? Did you kill somebody?'

He jerked his head back to look straight at her and she was appalled to realise that in trying to suggest the worst impossibility she had hit on some sort of truth.

Something was changing in his eyes as the strict guardian inside him, his last line of defence, tried to slam the doors on her.

She reached out and clasped both his hands in hers. Startled and vulnerable, he gripped them tightly.

Behind them, Maxwell, unsteady after four pints of beer and coming back to his tent for more money, said, 'Well, look at you two then.'

THE NEXT DAY, on the way in to breakfast, Patrick got a knowing smile from Gaye and a smirk from Maxwell. He walked round the back of the food tent to collect himself. Two of the other diggers were sitting on the grass behind it, a rabbity man called Martin and the woman with the huge trowel, whom CD had labelled Vera. Patrick had no idea whether that was her real name. They were chatting and didn't see him coming.

'. . . holding hands. He saw them. That's what he said.'

Patrick stopped again and turned back. With nowhere left to go, he went into the tent. Bobby gave him a wide smile. 'Good morning. How are you today?'

There were half a dozen people inside the tent assembling their breakfast. Patrick felt as if every eye was upon him.

'Oh,' he said, 'I'm fine.' Then out of embarrassment he said, far too abruptly, 'Can we get your tractor and trailer over quite soon, do you think? We need to get this lot moved as soon as possible.'

'Er, well, yes,' she said, disconcerted.

'Thanks,' he said, helped himself to coffee and cornflakes, and went outside without meeting her eye again.

All that day he kept away from her. He told himself that he was there as a professional, as a leader, and a leader should not be the butt of gossip.

It was a busy day, but by late afternoon it was all done, and the new camp was a much nicer place to be than the old one. They were just over the brow of the hill, fifty yards beyond the barrow on a small, almost flat plateau. The diggers cut the turf back to make a big campfire a safe distance from the site.

The site itself was another matter. CD and Dozer had looked at it closely as Patrick showed them what he had seen and where he had found the bead. CD tried the same trick, doing press-ups, but he looked less than convinced.

'Jeez, I hope you're right. I'm not sure I can see it.'

Patrick was already feeling his neck was stuck out way too far when the TV crew arrived, eager to start shooting.

'Can't you do a bit of planning or something?' Kenny Camden said, clearly disappointed that they weren't ready to start. 'What about you guys walking round deciding where to put the trench?'

This was something Patrick had intended to do by himself, but now it worked well. CD was in a generous mood again, and contributed some thoughtful ideas phrased in such a way that it sounded as if he was agreeing with something Patrick had already said.

'You're absolutely right,' he said. 'We need to do it in quadrants. If we start a trench about *here*'—he scratched a mark on the ground—'and take it through to say *here*'—another mark—'we should catch the edge of the ditch and get into the centre of the mound.'

They pegged the trench out, took careful measurements and called it a day. Queuing up for supper, Patrick made sure he was in animated conversation with CD about the need to get some proper paperwork together. He avoided looking directly at Bobby.

That night nobody went to the pub. Dozer, putting dirty dishes in the car for Bobby, said, 'Come on back after. We'll have a few bottles round the fire.'

She smiled at him and said she might, but she didn't.

They'd used the tractor to bring in a load of wood from the

farm, and round the blazing fire, fuelled by the wine, the diggers sang old Beatles songs, accompanied by CD on an improvised bongo made out of a catering tin of baked beans. Patrick almost enjoyed himself.

FIVE

By teatime on the first day of digging on the barrow, Patrick was getting sideways looks from the other diggers. Were his hopes unrealistic? He longed to see clear signs of a feature—a grave-shaped patch of different soil to prove that a later burial had taken place. What he saw, as he should have expected, was a horribly uniform surface of earth and small stones, and his doubts began to grow.

When Kenny Camden tried to get him to tell the camera what it was they were looking at, he couldn't put together any words that were halfway convincing. All they had found was an area of disturbance where rabbits had dug, and a couple of bullets.

Dozer twiddled one of the bullets between thumb and finger. 'Three-oh-three,' he said. 'World War Two, I reckon. Angle they were at, probably came from aircraft machine guns.'

Camden liked that and Dozer was encouraged to speculate on camera about the type of plane they might have been fired by.

'Spitfire, possibly,' he said, 'or a Hurricane.'

'Or someone out shooting foxes,' said Patrick under his breath.

'Always the romantic, eh, Dozer?' said CD.

'Hey, CD,' said Dozer, 'remember that time we were digging in Sumatra and I had to defuse that unexploded bomb?'

'No,' said CD, 'not Sumatra. That was Guadalcanal.'

Saved your life, though, didn't I?'

'Yeah, that's another one I owe you.'

Maxwell had stopped trowelling and sat back on his heels as he listened, goggle-eared, believing every word of it. Jack, the cameraman, smiled and switched off.

In the afternoon, just after the tea break, CD's bird made a painfully clumsy landing on Patrick's knee as he sat on a stool, writing up the trench records, and Patrick's pen and notebook fell in the grass. Edgar picked up the pen and flew off with it, landing on the grass a few steps away.

'Sorry,' said CD, running up. 'I'll get it. Good ravens don't do that, Edgar. Put it down.'

The jackdaw spread his wings, and disappeared into a large tree on the edge of the wood below.

'OK,' said CD, 'leave it with me. I know which tree it is.'

He and Patrick were stopped in their tracks by a bellow from Dozer. 'Over 'ere, you two.'

They walked back to the trench, where the other diggers were gathering around Dozer, gazing at the earth intently. They made a space for Patrick and CD.

Dozer, looking up at Patrick with an expression of proud ownership, said, 'Take a gander at this.' He was kneeling, and he put his face close to the earth to blow the loose soil away.

Showing through it was a flattened, irregular disc of rusty iron.

'Shield boss?' Patrick said.

'Looks like it,' said Dozer. 'There's your Saxon.'

Patrick's relief was enormous. It was the central part of a wooden shield and it increased to near certainty the chances that there had been a burial here. Then the satisfaction was overshadowed by a pang of regret. A shield meant a warrior. A warrior meant a man, not a woman. Whatever they had found, it was not the grave of the German Queen.

'Sorry, folks, I missed that,' said Jack, the cameraman. 'You couldn't do it again, could you?'

'How do you mean, do it again?'

'Well . . . just maybe put a bit of earth back over it and sort of, discover it again. Just for the pictures.'

They had to do it three times before he was sure he'd got it right. It went against everything Patrick had ever learned. You didn't mess about with contexts, not for the camera, not for anything. He was acutely uncomfortable and all the more so when they asked him to describe to the camera what they were looking at.

'It's an iron shield boss, more or less shaped like a cone.' He pointed out its shape in the soil. 'There should be a flange around its base with holes where it was attached to the wooden part of the shield.'

'Paddy, give us a bit about what this means,' ordered Kenny Camden. 'You know, what it tells you about the burial.'

'Turn the camera off,' snapped Patrick, furious. Camden turned and nodded at Jack.

'OK. Get this. Do *not* call me Paddy. If you do that to me on film, I'm not letting anyone do any more digging until you're out of here, understand?'

'Hey, listen. Calm down. Nobody's going to hear my words,' said Camden. 'We cut those. It'll just be you talking, right?'

'Ah. Well, just don't call me that, right?' said Patrick, discomfited.

When he'd calmed down, Patrick did his best, greatly helped by some asides from CD about the complexities of shield bosses.

'The shield boss,' said Patrick on the third take, 'indicates the probability that this is indeed an Anglo-Saxon burial site. It's the first important find we've made since we started digging and it's the right way up for a typical burial in which the shield might be laid flat, sometimes on the arm or across the chest. The design of these bosses developed steadily throughout the period, so it should help us date the burial fairly precisely. From what we can see of it so far, the shape looks as if it could be what's called a Group Six boss. That would date it from somewhere between the middle of the sixth century and the middle of the seventh.'

'Very good indeed,' said Camden.

'Nice one,' said Jack. 'I could do with a close-up.'

'Right,' said Camden. 'Can you just do that bit again.'

Patrick couldn't remember what he'd said so they had to play the tape to find out and he had to memorise his words. He was halfway through the fifth take when he ground to a halt.

'What's wrong now?' said Camden.

'Nothing,' said Patrick, looking intently at a small lump of soil. 'I think we've found bone.'

He pulled his trowel out of his back pocket and, with huge care, moved the soil out of the way, crumb by crumb, to expose unmistakable yellow-brown bone. The arm that had held the shield in battle still held it in death.

KENNY CAMDEN WAS delighted with the day's work when he and Jack drove off an hour later, leaving the diggers to put up a large square frame tent as a cover over the grave. At seventy-five miles an hour on the back road to Woodstock, Camden lit a cigar with both hands while he steered with his knees and Jack resented both the smoke and the risk the man was taking with their lives.

'Listen, Jacko,' Camden said, 'if we get another wobbly like that one, keep shooting, right? Even if he makes me agree to switch off, just pull out wide and keep the camera running. Act natural so he'll think it's off.'

'Mmm,' said Jack, who didn't much like being called Jacko either.

UNITED BY THE THRILL of having found something, eleven diggers gathered round the food tent that night in an extraordinarily cheerful mood. Six of the less enthusiastic volunteers had elected to quit when they moved to the new site and CD was missing. Sitting apart from the others, Patrick spun out the job of writing up the records. He was still on his guard with Bobby, feeling that any signs of friendliness he displayed could be misinterpreted, but he watched her when he thought no one was looking.

CD arrived as they were being handed bowls of a brown mixture that looked and smelt very like the previous day's stew. He was limping and dishevelled.

'Been in a fight?' said Dozer, looking hard at him.

'No,' he said, 'no, no, no. I walked into a door.'

'Dunno if you've noticed. This is the open air. It don't come fitted with doors.'

'Good point. Very good point. Couldn't have been a door then.'

'You've got a leaf in your hair. You been through a hedge?'

'Up a tree actually,' said CD, 'then down it again. Faster. Until I stopped. At the bottom.' He sat down and winced. 'Suddenly.'

'Not the tree where Edgar took my pen?' Patrick said. 'It wasn't anything special. You shouldn't have done it.'

'It's not just the pen,' said CD between gritted teeth. 'He took the keys to my Harley.'

'I'll sort it, mate,' said Dozer. 'Remember that time in Salisbury? I can crack a Harley lock in three seconds.'

‘I’d rather you didn’t,’ said CD stiffly. ‘That time, if you remember, you rode off on it too. I know exactly where my keys are. Believe me, that bird is in big, big trouble when he comes back.’

The meal was cleared away and nobody seemed inclined to move. It was a mellow evening. The diggers were sprawled on the grass. The wine had come out and CD and Dozer were telling old war stories.

‘So there we were, miles from sodding anywhere,’ Dozer was saying, ‘eight feet down in solid chalk, and this git sticks his head in the hole and says, “I say, my good men, this is han hancient monument. Hit his protected, don’t you know?” So old CD here, he looks up at the geezer and says, “Bugger off. We’re British Gas. We’re looking for a leak.” Worked like a charm.’

Patrick laughed, then caught a movement out of the corner of his eye and turned to find Bobby standing at his shoulder.

‘Could I have a word with you?’ she asked.

It seemed to him that silence had fallen. He suspected that they were all looking at him. ‘Of course you can. What about?’

‘Catering and things. I don’t want to break up the party. Shall we talk somewhere else?’

‘Right. Lead on.’

The last of the sun’s glow slipped from the base of the western clouds as they left the circle. Bobby walked ahead of him to the gate where the farm track started, then waited for Patrick to catch up.

‘Not here,’ she said. ‘Further away. Come to the house.’

Patrick walked down the hill after her in the deepening darkness. Ruts and potholes kept catching him out so that he fell further and further behind. Ahead, dark shapes of trees were fringed with light from the farmhouse beyond them and, as the track turned sharp left round a barn into thc entrance to the yard, he saw Bobby waiting for him. Only then did he belatedly realise that she was really angry.

He walked slowly up to her. ‘What’s wrong?’ he asked.

‘What’s wrong? I’ll tell you exactly what’s wrong,’ she said. ‘You seem to have singled me out specially for the cold-shoulder treatment and I must say I’m not quite sure what I’ve done to deserve it apart from listening to you last night. So what’s going on?’

What could he say? That he’d let his guard down and she had

slipped in under it? That he'd been embarrassed that others had seen his weakness? 'I . . . um, I made a bit of a fool of myself last night. When Maxwell came back and . . .'

'You mean he saw you upset and that's enough to make you think you have to be some kind of shitty, aloof bastard to me all day?'

'I didn't mean to—'

'You didn't mean to treat me like I wasn't there? Like I was some sort of scullery maid? What sort of person are you? Why do you have to be some great big macho iceberg all the time?'

'It's not that. Maxwell spread it around. I heard everybody talking this morning. They think . . . we've got something going.'

'Oh I see.' She nodded a couple of times. 'So because of that, you think it's all right to behave in this stupid way all day?'

He sat down on the edge of a stone trough and put his head in his hands. 'I'm sorry. I'm very, very sorry. You're right.'

She sat down next to him. 'What is wrong with you?' she said and the words sounded much less harsh. 'You stand out like a sore thumb. Just relax a bit. Stop putting yourself out in the cold.'

'I'm not very good at authority. I need to be in charge here. That's what I'm here for. It doesn't come naturally.'

'You don't do it that way. You can be yourself. If you're halfway reasonable with people, they'll respect you.'

'Oh God. Believe me, I can't be myself. That's one thing I'm trying very hard not to be.'

'What does that mean?'

'I don't think I can talk about it.'

'Patrick, I think you *have* to.'

Side by side, two feet apart, he could look straight ahead and not be disturbed by her face.

'I lost someone.'

'Well, yes. I know that.'

'How do you know?'

'I found out. You may have forgotten but you were quite famous. I looked you up on the Internet. There's pages and pages about you.'

'Are there?' He was genuinely astonished.

'Of course there are. Every song you ever did. Pictures of you on stage. Reams and reams of stuff about you quitting your band.

It says you had a wife. It says no one knew until you quit.'

'When I quit,' he repeated softly, 'I didn't have a wife any more.'

As if she knew the shape but not the precise nature of the jagged tear in his soul, she skirted round the obvious question.

'Why didn't anyone know about her?'

'The record company didn't want them to. They want people like me to be an object of lust. I got married young. Rachel . . .' There, he'd said her name out loud. 'Rachel was too . . . I don't know. Normal? Not glamorous. Anyway, she got in the way, they said, so they told the world I was single. It was just plain dumb.'

'Did she mind?'

'I think she minded every single thing that happened to her from then on.'

'Patrick,' said Bobby. 'What happened in Perugia?'

'What do you know about Perugia?' He sensed her flinch away from him.

'All it says is that you quit your band in Perugia, after a concert. It says what happened was tied up with . . . well, I don't know. Something pretty bad. Was that when Rachel left you?'

He stood up. 'Enough. That's enough.'

'Patrick, I just want to help.'

'Look, Bobby, it doesn't help. I don't want to go there. You think this is good for me. I know what's safe and this isn't safe and it's me who has to live with it, not you. We've got a dig to do, thanks to Joe. That's all I'm going to think about.'

'All right,' she said helplessly.

'I've heard what you said and I'm sorry I upset you. I'll try to treat you exactly like I treat everybody else from now on.'

THE TRACK ROSE over the fold of the hill and, a hundred yards ahead, the campfire bloomed—black backs in front, orange flames and yellow faces beyond.

Patrick stopped at the field gate and stared towards the fire and wished from the bottom of his soul that he could turn the clock back and just be one of them, a normal person with a normal history of no great interest to anyone. He'd only been fooling himself by thinking he had managed to duck out of the spotlight for ever.

Perugia was his private hell, not another peg for public speculation, spread round the world by cybergossip.

In Perugia he had watched the little boy playing in the cathedral light. He had seen the boy's father sit down on a bench and watch the child, smiling in unhurried tolerance. Patrick, in an anguish of repentance for what he had done on stage the night before on worldwide television—and coming down from the effects of the chemical cocktails of the past twenty-four hours—had seen how a boy and his father should be. He had seen the little boy lost in his simple world. He had seen the boy's father respecting that world and giving him all the time he needed, centring his day on his child and not himself. In that moment, Patrick had vowed to be a better father to David and a better husband to Rachel.

Along the far wall had been a row of confessionals, open-fronted, priests sitting inside in full view. Patrick longed to confess but he had no God to confess to. He closed his eyes and made his confession to himself, but it came out with excuses attached. I've been selfish, he said to the listener inside his head . . . I needed the space. I've betrayed the people I care about most . . . but she's pushed me into it. She hasn't understood where I have to go.

Something about the place he was in stopped him, blocked his evasions and brought him closer to the inescapable truth that if he was to save anything from this, if he was to give David all he wanted to give him, then he had to leave the band. He had no choice but to walk out of the cathedral to where he had left the band's manager, Don Claypole, sitting at a restaurant table on the edge of the square.

He had headed for Don to tell him it was all over, finished. He didn't care if it cost him all the money he had. He would get Rachel back from the wasteland in which he had thrust her. For David's sake.

The scene was clear in Patrick's memory and always would be. His eyes protested at the bright lunchtime light. Coming up the steps towards him through the dazzle was a dark figure saying in Don Claypole's voice, 'Ah, Paddy, there you are,' and Patrick was saying back to him, 'Don, I've got something to tell you,' and the man replied, 'No, mate, I've got something to tell you first.'

He was pulled out of his memories by a figure coming towards him. 'Patrick? What are you doing out here? Did you sort things out with Bobby?'

'Er, yes.'

'Right.' CD leaned on the gate next to him and there was a long silence. 'Happy?' said the American in the end.

'God, what a question.'

'You want to hear what my mammy taught me?' He went on without waiting for an answer. 'She taught me not to leave my rocks near any hard places. Also to avoid animals with horns in case they turned out to be savage dilemmas. And to beat some other guy's back, not my own.'

Silence from Patrick, not trusting himself to reply.

'You've got to learn to zigzag. You got to know your snakes from your ladders. If you go one step forward and two steps back, you just say that's great, I'm waltzing, yeah?'

A small grunt came that could have been assent or amusement.

'OK,' said CD, 'that's good. You're in there somewhere. Now, let's talk about this.'

'It's late.' Everyone wanted to talk. Except him.

'It's only six o'clock on the East Coast. No need to panic. I'm only talking archaeology here. I guess that's allowed?' CD saw Patrick give a little nod. 'So, let's look at this guy we're digging up. He was born. He died. A thousand years later all we have left is the hard bits and a few knick-knacks. Maybe he was a happy guy. Maybe he was a sad old Saxon git. We sure as hell can't tell and he tasted the same to the worms. In the end it made no difference. The world still turns. You only get one chance and you might as well be happy. In the end, no one gives a shit.'

'I know it's silly, but I hoped it would be a woman,' said Patrick.

'Me too,' said CD. 'Maybe there's a woman there as well.'

'Unlikely. This one looks like it's dead centre in the barrow.'

'Well, dead, anyway. I did some digging in France,' said CD thoughtfully. 'Champagne-Ardenne. We found these incredible burials—men and women together. Some of them were holding hands. Some had their arms round each other. We all cried like babies. Dozer was there. Ex-President of the Hell's Angels and there he was, down on his knees, tears pouring down his face.'

'He really was a Hell's Angel? I thought that was just a story you made up for Roger Little.'

'No, no. He was the Boss, the toughest of the tough. Even back then, when he was still biking, he used to go on digs. Been digging since he was twelve. Two sides to his life.'

'We're not going to find another burial in the barrow.'

'I guess not. So much for our friend and his song about the German Queen. Shame. I would have liked to find the chicken blade.'

Patrick laughed.

'Hey, anyway, Patrick. We could do something for these diggers, you and I. Make it more real. Every night when the cameras have gone, we could do a bit of speculating round the campfire for fun, pin some humanity on those old bones.'

'I don't see why not.' Patrick looked up. The crowd round the fire was thinning out. His devils had left him and he felt drained and inexpressibly weary. 'Time for bed,' he said.

'OK,' agreed CD, content that his prime objective had been met. Bringing Patrick and his team together for a nightly session round the fire might help bridge the chasm between them. It might also help take away the pained, distracted vacancy in Patrick's eyes.

ONCE AGAIN IT WAS Dozer who made the next find, soon after they started in the morning. Kneeling on planks stretched across the trench, the huge man was gently teasing the grains of soil out from where the shield would have been, exposing the rib cage below. There, lying across two of the ribs, was a large circular object eight inches across. It was encrusted with dirt and corrosion, but at its edges intricately decorated metal gave away its origins, which were, quite clearly, much older than the shield.

Patrick had entrusted the main job to his most experienced diggers, CD and Dozer working on the area around the shield boss while the others were kept out of the way, extending the other trench towards the edges of the barrow. They all spent as much of their time as they decently could looking enviously towards the two men digging in the centre of the mound.

Finding the disc brought work to a complete halt and took Kenny Camden, who arrived just in time to see its uncovering, to the point of rapture. For Patrick, the trouble started when Peter Knight looked at what they'd found and confirmed his fears.

'Look at the edge decoration,' Peter said. 'That's not Anglo-Saxon, is it? Roman, surely.'

CD agreed and after a quick and disturbing conference between the two of them Patrick had to find something sensible to say for the camera.

'This is, um, definitely a bit of a surprise,' he said in the end. 'It's not at all the sort of thing you would expect to find with an Anglo-Saxon burial. It appears to be Roman . . .' After that he just trailed off into silence.

'What do you think it is?' Camden prompted, off camera.

'I haven't a clue. We'll have to get it cleaned before we know.'

'Look, Pad—Patrick, you've got to say *something* that makes a bit more sense than that. Viewers expect some sort of narrative. You can't just duck out.'

'But we *don't* have a clue. It's completely unexpected.'

'OK, well say so, but do it with a bit more force.'

Patrick had another go. 'This has come out of the blue. We don't know what it is yet. It needs a lot of cleaning but it's clearly highly decorated—some sort of plaque perhaps, apparently laid across the chest in the burial. The strangest thing of all is that it is very obviously not Anglo-Saxon. Our best guess at the moment is that it's Roman workmanship so what it's doing here, in the middle of this burial, is a complete mystery.'

'Very good,' said Camden. 'Just the ticket. How soon can we get it cleaned up?'

'Well, that's up to John Hescroft. That would be part of the post-exploration. When we've finished. If there's any money.'

'No, no, no. That won't do. I'll sort it out.' Camden started tapping numbers into his mobile phone, walking off towards his car. When he came back he had a triumphant grin on his face.

'Hescroft's fixed it. The lab is going to get stuck into it straight away. He said you'd know where to take it. I'm getting a good buzz out of this. We could be onto a good one.'

When the heavy Roman disc had been carefully lifted from the trench, Patrick took it into Oxford and saw it safely into the hands of the conservation specialists.

It was after five when he drove back into Wytchlow. Unwilling to dive straight back into the life of the dig, he took the right fork down the side of the village green and pulled into a small lay-by at the end of a pathway up to the church.

It proved to be old and simple, a mixture of Norman and Gothic. Inside it was full of spring flowers, sprays of white and yellow, and as Patrick looked at them a clear memory came back to him from the weeks immediately after Perugia. The weeks he had wandered through Britain's lonely places, seeking isolation, explanation and then finally, obliteration.

He'd escaped the press siege, had his head completely shaved, and had swapped his Mercedes for a small camper van. He'd headed north, driving into the night until he was deep into Northumberland. He went to sleep in a car park on the coast with no idea where he was. At seven, he looked out to find himself under the walls of Bamburgh Castle. He gazed out across the beach to where the waves were breaking on the Farne Islands and saw a place where he could make a grand, silent end of himself.

For the next two days it was as if he was counting down to that final moment, going over his entire life in detail, clearing the decks for that one-way swim that seemed the only remaining possibility.

What saved him was an extraordinary event on Holy Island.

He had waited at the landward end of the causeway until the tide's retreat let the first gleam of the road surface show through between the waves. Then he drove onto Holy Island, a low place of rough grass and sand dunes, a halfway halt between one world and another.

He left the camper and walked to Lindisfarne Castle on the seaward side where the waves exerted a hypnotic pull, roaring and frothing over the reefs. Last of all, he turned into the ruined priory.

Its miraculous archway, still arcing across from pillar to pillar where all the rest had fallen, came to him briefly as an omen, a signal that in all great ruins something precious may still sustain. The moment was immediately spoilt by the influx of a horde of tourists, a shrill army wrapped in bright plastic. To avoid them, he hurried into the tiny church that stood facing the priory ruins.

Inside, an old man in vicar's black smiled at him and, getting no response, left him to himself. Patrick sat on a pew. He could still find no God to talk to, no God to stop him, only his unbearable self and the trail of damage he had left. It seemed to him that he had committed a sin that was irredeemable, that the crucified Christ on the altar might well have died for sinners but not for sinners as bad as he.

Then, signalling the end of quiet thought, the entire group of sightseers, noisy as gulls and dripping wet, streamed into the narrow aisles. He got up and headed for the door. He reached the back of the church but got no further. A group of seven or eight teenagers burst in noisily, dressed in exuberant rags. In the lead was a girl with a face of fragile beauty and purposeful intent but her cohorts, all boys, had eyes that seemed to Paddy to be accustomed to trouble. As they made their way towards the altar, the vicar watched anxiously, prepared to try to stop them if they attempted to abscond with the candlesticks. But that was not their intention at all. They filed into the front pew and knelt to pray, then after a few seconds the girl stood up, framed by the white flowers in vases in the archway ahead of her. She held her hands out to each side and turned her face up towards the ceiling. The boys next to her got up and, as she let loose a long high note, they joined in, singing in harmony to some ancient unfamiliar tune, with words in a foreign language. It was a song of soaring power and at the end there were little noises of appreciation right through the church.

The girl turned and came back down the aisle, followed by the boys. The vicar put out a hand and stopped her.

'My dear,' he said, 'where are you from?'

'From the old eastern part of Germany,' she said.

'What you just did was very special,' said the old man. 'Would you tell me why you did it?'

'This is my brother,' she said, 'and these are my cousins, and since we were born we did not see each other until the Wall came down. I made a promise that if my brother and I could see our cousins, I would one day make . . . what is it? *Eine Wallfahrt*.'

'A pilgrimage?'

'Yes, I think so. I said I would come here and give thanks and that is what I have done.'

'Why here?'

'Oh. I had a postcard on my wall for all the years, a very old postcard of your church and your beautiful island. I always was thinking that it looked a good place for new beginnings.'

Paddy, seeking only an ending, left the church, striding out past the priory ruins to the rocks where the waves waited. He sat down to stare at the sea until the moment of certainty came, but what came instead was the German girl, following him in concern. She sat down beside him and asked him what it was that troubled him. While her brothers and cousins kept a distant watch, she listened with intense concentration as he unaccountably told her the whole story. Then, instead of anything banal, she nodded and said that, yes, the waves might be a perfectly good choice under such circumstances but it was hard to be sure because the future is not written yet and perhaps he had a lot to give in exchange for all that he had taken.

'You are right. You have done bad things. Better to throw away just that part of you, not the whole of you. And if you drown yourself here you will spoil my special place for me and I will never be able to look at my postcard again.'

Then she kissed him on the cheek and went back to her family while he sat on his rock and found that the impulse to self-destruction had now acquired a counterbalance. He walked along the seaward shore, taking a new interest in the shape and sound and smell of things. He was surprised when the Germans showed up that afternoon at the campsite near Berwick-upon-Tweed, but if he'd been watching in his mirror he would have seen their van shadowing him.

After that, by common agreement, they had continued in convoy for the next week, wandering through the Lammermuir Hills, spending time walking, sitting and talking. The boys' English wasn't nearly as good as the girl's so she and Patrick spent most of that time talking together. She was called Beatriz, and she fanned the faint embers of his past enthusiasms, forcing him to dredge his memory for facts about the history of the land they were in. Eventually she found his true centre—archaeology.

'You care about these things,' she said. 'Maybe you should go back to take an interest in them. It will, I think, help you to heal. You have no god you recognise, so believe in something. Go on digging.'

They had all driven together back to Harwich and, when he waved them off as the ferry sailed away, he was back from the brink and set on the path that led him to this new life.

WHEN PATRICK RETURNED to the hilltop, by some TV-influenced miracle the site had acquired some of the trappings of a proper dig during his absence. A small hut had been delivered to protect the finds and a portable shower unit now stood next to the loos. Bobby served another variation on the theme of brown stew and mashed potatoes but they swallowed it with enthusiasm. Even Gaye ate it. Until now, she had been picking at the food then eating secret supplies in her tent.

Bobby sat down at the table opposite Patrick.

'You're eating with us tonight, then,' he said.

She raised her eyebrows and smiled. 'Looks like it. CD told us about the discussion session and I thought I'd like to be here.'

Temporarily, in the low light of early evening, she wasn't so like Rachel. The evening sun accentuated the planes of her face—more curved than Rachel's. Or perhaps, he thought, it's just that Bobby looks serene and Rachel never did.

'When are we starting?' she asked.

Everyone always thought he had a plan. He had no plans.

'I don't know. When we've cleared the table?'

They washed up using cold water from a newly erected standpipe and then they got the campfire going. Patrick found himself facing an expectant ring of faces. With his mind a blank, he looked for CD to rescue him, but the American sat there smiling amiably back at him with all the rest, his bird perched on his shoulder.

'OK,' Patrick said. 'Um, I thought we might, er . . . Well, we might go over what happened today and, well, you know, talk about it.'

Lame start, he thought.

'As you're all aware, we found an object this morning that doesn't quite make sense. We know this is an Anglo-Saxon burial.'

Aidan put up his hand. 'How do we know?' he said in his direct way.

'Well, we found the shield boss. It's typical of a particular period.'

'Yes, but now you've found something Roman so maybe it's the shield boss that shouldn't be there. Maybe someone buried the shield there later, on top of a Roman burial?'

'Well, the Romans didn't usually bury people in the middle of old barrows. That's definitely more of a Saxon thing.'

'What is this Roman thing anyway?' asked Gaye.

'It's too early to tell,' said Patrick. 'We'll have to—'

'You're always saying that,' cut in Maxwell. ' Too early to tell.'

CD smiled. 'That's the way it is, kid. You better learn those words. It's archaeologists' speak for I don't have any idea and I'm not going to guess until I have to. Consider yourself privileged to be here tonight for a rare event. This is guessing time. Tonight we can all stick our necks out. Just don't hold it against us when we're wrong.'

'So let's hear your guess then,' said Gaye.

'OK,' said CD. 'It's more or less round. It's too big and heavy to be a brooch and it looks too lumpy to be any kind of dish or plate. I think it's most probably a clutch-plate for an early Roman Chevrolet.'

'Early Roman Chevrolets had automatic gearboxes,' said Peter. 'It looks more like a Ford to me.' His face was deadpan and it was a moment before the laughter started.

'Some kind of medallion, ain't it, Pat?' said Dozer. 'Something a bit ceremonial. Looked kind of like that to me.'

'It's too . . .' started Patrick, and the rest of them joined in a chorus, '. . . early to tell.'

They all burst out laughing and Patrick joined in. With delight, CD watched his scheme starting to work.

'Supposing it is an Anglo-Saxon burial . . .' said Bobby's rich voice from the growing darkness beyond the fire. 'And supposing this other thing is Roman. He could have found it, couldn't he? Maybe he just liked old things so they buried it with him.'

'I dunno,' said Dozer. 'They didn't 'ave time to go collecting then, did they? Shelter and food and not getting a spear between the shoulder blades, that's what they thought about mostly.'

'Bullshit, Doze,' said CD amiably. 'They made beautiful things, those guys. Look at the Alfred jewel or the Kingston Down brooch. They knew about beauty. Why couldn't they collect it? Maybe this guy found it when he was digging up potatoes one day and thought, Hey, cool. I'll keep that to be buried with.'

'They didn't 'ave potatoes, you dopey four-eyed git,' Dozer said. 'Thought you'd know that, you being a clever clogs with a college education.'

'Oh right, so that invalidates my whole thesis, I guess. Potatoes, turnips, whatever. Go sick him, Edgar.'

The jackdaw flapped onto Dozer's head.

'I give in,' said the big man. 'No call to start bringing in air support. Call your effing vulture off. 'Ere, Bobby. Can't your Joe sing us another song? Tell us what's going on?'

'Joe sings when he wants to,' said Bobby. 'I can't tell him to. I don't even know where he is tonight.' But she looked round and stared into what was now full darkness on the hilltop.

'Of course the real question,' said CD, 'is why do we like all this old shit anyway? Who do we—? Whoa there, hang on just a minute. Was that a bottle I heard? The gentle slopping of some sublime liquid in a vessel of the clearest crystal? Is that the product of a far-off fermentation that I smell over there in the darkness beyond the fire? I think it's singing to me. Come on, bottle. Come to daddy. Cast your Glenboggy on the waters as they say and it shall be returned threefold.'

Bottles emerged from the shadows. Wine began to circulate. Then Aidan said, 'Go on, then, what's the answer?'

'Answers? I don't have answers. I have enough trouble with the questions,' said CD. 'You know how it is: you pull a lump of Samian ware out of the ground and you're the first person to see it since some Roman matron smashed it in the year 300. That's half the thrill, but you look at it carefully because it might just be some kind of pattern nobody's ever seen before and then everyone will be saying "CD? Sure, isn't he the guy who first identified the Samian ware toothbrush steriliser?".'

'I can imagine that Anglo-Saxon finding his Roman clutch-plate,' said Patrick, speaking with no conscious effort from out of the reverie of thought CD had led him into. 'He wouldn't know where it came from, would he? He probably wouldn't even know how it was made. Maybe it seemed like magic.'

It was the first completely unforced sentence he had uttered in four years, but before that dawned on him a guitar chord came out of the darkness behind the fire and every head swivelled towards the sound.

'Come and join us,' CD called.

When the guitar sounded again, it was much easier to hear, but the person playing it was still all but invisible to them. When he started to sing, the voice was Joe's.

The tune was what they all wanted to hear—the song of the German Queen. This time, Joe started somewhere in the middle.

'A month went by while they mourned the son
And marked the great deeds he had done
By laying his shield across his chest
As they put him in the grave to rest.

That was when they came again
In the storm-dark night, those murderous men,
Feet wrapped in cloth and swords honed keen
But they didn't allow for the German Queen.

She stayed awake while her brothers slept.
Moon-shadows moved in the watch she kept
And when she heard a skittering stone,
She beat the gong with a great leg bone.

Three brothers only faced the foe
And they made their stand by the witch's low.
They stood surrounded, back to back,
Against the waves of the night attack.

Their sister raced to summon aid,
To bring the King with his chicken blade.
But the King's old legs brought him too late.
His last three sons had met their fate.

The King's hot blade was slaked in blood.
Six traitors lay in the red-striped mud.
Down that hill they bore their own
And buried them round their valley home.

The King turned to his daughter dear
And spoke to her of his dreadful fear.
"You, my Queen, are the only one
Left of my line. You must bear a son."'

Joe seemed to falter there, playing an extended instrumental passage, stopping and starting again as if uncertain where to pick up the tale. Then he came to a decision and launched into a new verse but it was clear he had jumped ahead in the story.

'At the village under the witch's low
The Queen and her children came to know
A time of peace, a time to mend,
A time they thought would never end.

She filled their home with the things she found
Given up by the riven ground,
Sharp axes chipped from ancient stone,
A stag's head carved from an old thigh bone.

When others shunned the Romans' stones
She dared inspect their resting bones
And there, when winter turned to spring
She found what proved her favourite thing.

What came to her from the deer-delved earth
As if the land had given birth
What she saw beneath the sod
Was the leafy brow of the woven god.'

There followed another long pause. When, eventually, the silence stretched too far, one of the diggers swung the beam of his powerful torch around the field but Joe was nowhere to be seen.

'What's a woven god?' said Aidan.

'I haven't a clue,' Patrick replied.

'I thought he said "Woden god",' said Maxwell. 'That would make more sense, wouldn't it? Wasn't there a god called Woden? Or maybe he said "wooden". A wooden god.'

'A hell of a story,' said Aidan.

'Come on,' Gaye said. 'It's obvious he knows we found something today and he's made it up. No offence, Bobby. But you don't want to start putting any faith into things like that.'

'Hang about, Gaye. You stop being the cynic,' said Dozer. 'That's my job. It's what I'm known for, good looks and cynicism.'

'And your slim figure, I suppose?' she scoffed.

'Even if Gaye's right,' said CD, 'he's a hell of a songwriter. Hears us talking and makes up a song to fit just like that.'

'Doesn't fit though, does it?' said Dozer. 'He's still going on about a her. What we've got here is a him.'

'Come on, Bobby,' said Maxwell. 'What's it all about?'

'Oh, don't ask me. He's my brother and he's a good man, but I don't know how his mind works. I'm sure that he always has the best of reasons for what he does. I think maybe it's some sort of parable.'

'What does that mean?'

'Well, I don't mean this to sound disloyal to him. What I mean is I don't suppose it's meant to be literally true. The axes and the stag's head in that last bit of the song, I know where they come from. They're on our mantelpiece at home.'

'There you are,' said Gaye.

'What sort of axes?' said CD.

'Old hand axes. My father used to collect old bits and pieces. People say he was a great one for seeing things. He'd walk the fields after ploughing and he'd bend down and pick up stuff nobody else could even see. He knew what he was looking for.'

'Didn't you know him? You said "people say".'

'He died when I was pretty young. My mother and Joe ran the farm after that. Joe was almost sixteen then. I was a bit of an afterthought. Then, when my mother died, I came in with Joe because he does need a bit of looking after. Not domestically, but business things. I mean he doesn't talk on the phone. That makes life a bit difficult.'

Patrick had been staring at Bobby, fascinated. 'So your father was a bit of an antiquarian?'

'Oh yes. The trouble is I often don't know what the things are.'

'You could take them to the museum.'

'There's not a lot of seconds left over in a struggling farmer's day for that sort of thing,' she said wryly. 'I know I'm taking time off to come up here but that counts as my first holiday for five years.'

'It's not exactly a holiday, is it?' said Patrick, feeling suddenly that they had all been taking her efforts rather for granted.

Dozer broke in. 'Someone's coming,' he said, and certainly a torch was probing in their direction from the track.

'Hello there. Are you the diggers?' called a querulous male voice.

'No, we're Diana Ross and the Supremes,' said Dozer.

'Yes, we are,' Patrick called back quickly.

The figure came up to the fire, shining the torch directly into Patrick's eyes. 'Are you the feller in charge?' said the new arrival.

'Yes. I'm Patrick Kane.'

'I'm the Reverend Augustus Templeton-Jones,' said the new arrival, finally switching off the torch.

'What can we do for you?'

'I heard that you might be in need of my services.'

'In what way?' asked Patrick, puzzled.

'You've found a body, I understand.'

So the news had got out already. One or two of the diggers had been down to the village shop. They must have told someone.

'We've found a possible burial, yes.'

'May I take it that you are going to observe proper procedures?'

'I'm not sure I know what you mean.'

'Oh, I'm sure you do, Mr Kane. As you will know, it is a requirement that any Christian remains that are disinterred should be given proper Christian reburial, at the earliest suitable opportunity.'

'Reverend, er . . .' Patrick couldn't begin to remember his name. 'What we have here is almost certainly a pre-Christian burial. I'd say it's probably sixth- or seventh-century Anglo-Saxon and—'

'Augustine came to Kent in the year 597, young man. Correct me if I'm wrong but that was the sixth century.'

From the darkness, a voice, Peter Knight's, said, 'St Birinus didn't convert Cynegils of the Gewisse until around 639 and this would be on the fringe of the Gewisse's territory. There was, of course, the pagan reaction to Christianity during the reign of Æthelbert's son, Eadbald, to take into account.'

Someone clapped quietly.

'In any case,' said Patrick, 'this grave doesn't show the usual signs of Christianity. It's not orientated east–west. The evidence so far is that it's a pagan burial.'

'Well, that would suit some of my parishioners,' said the vicar with a sniff. 'I doubt you can be certain, however, and if there is any doubt then I shall insist on all the proper ceremonies being carried out.'

'Scuse me, governor,' put in Dozer. 'If it's not a Christian, is it all right if we just chuck the bones in a box?'

'That would be a matter entirely for you,' said the vicar.

'Suppose it's a Roman?'

'As I say, that would be a matter entirely for you.'

'But weren't most of the Romans Christians?'

'I think you're trying to trip me up,' said the vicar crossly, and turned on Patrick. 'Have you informed the Coroner's Office of your find? That is a requirement when you unearth human remains.'

'Well, I know it is in theory. In practice, they tend to get a bit annoyed if you ring them up about bodies that have been dead for over a thousand years.'

'I can see that none of you can be trusted to follow proper procedures,' said the vicar. 'I shall be keeping a very close eye on your activities. I bid you good night.' He turned away, switched on his torch and stumbled over a rabbit hole, to the barely suppressed delight of the diggers round the fire.

'Why is it that the words "total dickhead" somehow spring effortlessly to mind?' said CD when he'd gone.

'That's the man I told you about,' said Bobby. 'The one who's causing all the trouble at the school over the May Morning procession.'

'Would you like him killed?' said Dozer. 'I've got a mate does it on the side. He's a fancy cake chef the rest of the time.'

'No, thank you, Dozer. It's very kind.'

'He's right about the burials, you know,' said CD. 'If it's Christian, you have to do it right. I was doing all the post-ex on a dig last year. We hit the edge of the old paupers' burial ground in Saintsbrook. Two hundred and ten bodies. I went along to the crematorium and asked if they did a cheap deal for more than one body, but it still came to twenty grand.'

'What did you do?'

'Found a friendly vicar and put them all in a big hole when they were doing his drains.'

'So what's going to happen to our bloke here then?' asked Maxwell.

'There'll be tests to do. We look at his bones and decide what killed him and if he had any diseases, then they go in a box somewhere in case anybody wants to have another look at them later on.'

'Unless he's a Christian.'

'If he's a Christian, I'm a boiled egg,' said CD.

'I'd better go,' said Bobby. 'You don't want to be kept waiting for your breakfast in the morning.'

'Up the revolution,' said CD. 'Anything we can do to help, just say the word.'

She stood looking towards where Patrick and CD sat, and the light from the low fire painted her a new face. 'Thanks. Come and join the May Day march. It's next week.' Then she was gone.

'She's a great kid,' said CD. 'I didn't know farmers came with built-in beauty and culture. Maybe I should be a farmer. I could marry her and settle down.'

'Nah, she wouldn't 'ave you,' said Dozer. 'Anyone can tell she's only got eyes for one bloke.'

'Who's that then?'

'Me, of course,' said Dozer. 'You're too effing ugly.'

Before they all turned in for the night, someone started singing the inevitable campfire songs and CD noticed with satisfaction that Patrick sang along with them, though he kept his voice so low they could barely hear him.

EARLY THE NEXT DAY, Patrick dressed and crawled out of his tent into dew-laden grass. There was a gauze curtain across the land but the sun was already warm and a lark's song was sparkling down through the spring air. The mist would not last. He walked straight to the mound and found that someone had been there before him. A tin can sat on the grass next to the trench and in it was a bunch of wild flowers. He lifted the grave cover off carefully and the bones curved out of the earth, just the forearm and a few ribs so far, the merest hint of the complex person whose framework this was.

A shadow fell across the earth. He twisted, startled, and an accusing ghost had climbed up out of the mist, staring at him.

Rachel reached out to touch his arm and said in a voice that was not Rachel's, 'Patrick. It's all right. It's me, Bobby. I just wanted to come up while it was still quiet. I didn't think anyone would be here.'

'We're not the first.' He pointed at the flowers. 'Was that Joe?'

'Maybe. I don't know. It's not like him.' She tilted her head. 'Do you think we'll uncover the rest of the body today?'

'You have to take things like this very slowly,' he said. 'Bones may look strong but they can crumble on you just like that. If the soil's too acid they get eaten away. It's quite dry and chalky here but it's not like that all the way through. There's a wet patch at the end of the other trench. I think maybe you've got a spring or something.'

'These bones look quite strong.'

'I hope so.'

'Thank you for last night,' she said. 'Will you go on doing the discussions?'

'Maybe. I will if Joe comes again. Those songs are extraordinary.'

'I'm glad you think so. He's not being a nuisance?'

'Anything that makes the Maxwells of this world think is not a nuisance.'

'Are you enjoying this dig, Patrick?'

'Enjoying it? I suppose I am. At least I'm starting to.'

'I'd better go and get the kettles on.'

She was gone and the mist was lifting. He looked after her and found he *was* enjoying it. For a man who fully expected never to enjoy anything, this came as a surprise.

CAMDEN AND HIS CAMERAMAN arrived two hours after the group started digging. Earlier, over breakfast, Dozer had got a metal detector out of his car and had run it over the spoil heap. 'Just checking,' he had said.

It buzzed and he dug around with his trowel until he found a small lump of earth with a metal edge showing.

'Well, that's a pity,' he said, bringing it back to the tent.

They all gathered round.

'Which of you threw it away, I wonder.'

'Why are you looking at me?' said Maxwell.

It might have been a pendant or a fragment of a brooch and seemed to have three short arms, one of them folded over where something had hit it. Describing it for the camera took half an hour.

'Could it be a cross?' Camden asked while Jack was filming.

'It's just possible. One of the arms could have been cut off. We won't know until it's been cleaned.' Patrick waited until he saw the camera switched off. 'Anyway, don't tell the vicar.'

He took Camden on one side. 'Look, if we have to keep stopping because you're not here when we find things, this could take years.'

'Paddy old son—'

'Patrick, please.'

'Patrick. Ease up. You know how it is with filming. Anyway, I'm the bearer of good news. I'm well on the way to getting proper money fixed up, a real budget for the pilot. If your boss agrees, we can both throw in a bit more, and then I can arrange things for you. More lab work. Whatever.'

'So long as you get what you want for the show?'

'We're going the same way, you and me. You want to find interesting things. So do I. If it needs a bit of cash to get them cleaned or whatever, we're up for it. That's all I'm saying.'

'Hescroft hasn't agreed to this yet, then?'

'Well, not yet, but you and I, we can persuade him, can't we?'

While this conversation was going on, CD had left the trench and strolled over, waiting politely for them to finish.

'Did you want something?' Camden said.

'Just a word with the boss,' CD said. 'Private matter.'

'Sounds interesting,' said Camden.

'Yes, it is. It's Maxwell. He's got terrible diarrhoea, so I was thinking, in case it spreads we should get a stool sample and send it off for analysis, so I need a jar and—'

'I'll leave you to it,' said Camden.

When he'd gone, Patrick looked at CD. 'What?' he said.

'Smoke screen. Well, more like riot gas really. Worked, didn't it? I need to tell you something and I didn't want him to hear until you had a chance to think about it. We've found more bones.'

'Yes?' said Patrick, thinking that was what you might expect when you were digging up a skeleton. 'So?'

'You'd better see for yourself.'

When Dozer saw the two of them walking back, he got out of the trench, beckoned Camden over to him, said something and then walked off with him towards the Land Cruiser where Jack was doing something to his equipment.

'He's running interference for us,' said CD. 'Good old Doze.'

They reached the mound.

'OK,' CD called, 'early coffee break. Cover up your loose.'

The diggers went without a backward glance and the hairs on the back of Patrick's neck began to prickle. Finds were usually announced immediately. These people had no idea that CD and Dozer had come across anything out of the way.

The cover was back over the skeleton and to start with CD left it in place. 'First off, let me walk you through the way it's gone. We've uncovered the side of the skull, all the rib cage and enough of the legs to be pretty sure the body is lying supine, with the arms crossed at the wrists over the pelvis. The skull's tilted to one side and we've exposed the top surface of the pelvis.'

'Sounds fine.'

'Well, it's not.' CD sounded rattled. 'Take a good look.'

He lifted the frame away carefully and Patrick stared down at what was now a recognisable skeleton, partly emerging from a bed of soil. At a quick glance there was nothing else to see.

'I don't see any extra bones,' he said. 'What do you mean?'

'You have to get down close.'

'OK.' Patrick knelt on the soil.

‘Look just above the pelvis,’ said CD.

When Patrick tuned his gaze, he saw two tiny bones, thinner than the thinnest part of a chicken’s wishbone, rearing out of the earth.

‘Oh, I see. Rodent?’ said Patrick. ‘Could be rabbit ribs.’

‘Those bones are not from an animal. They’re human.’

‘Oh, come on. They’re far too small. They’re like a baby’s . . .’ Patrick’s voice died away.

‘They’re exactly like a baby’s,’ said CD, ‘because that’s what they are. This warrior of ours was pregnant. Congratulations, young Patrick. Against all odds, we seem to have found the German Queen.’

Patrick stared at him, then back at the frail bones. Elation was quickly followed by a sense of something approaching horror. This was something unique in archaeological history. It meant that this was a huge dig, one that would have to be done just right. On the other hand, there was Joe’s song . . . so much that couldn’t be explained. Archaeology was science. Joe’s song seemed more like magic. The two could not easily coexist.

‘What do we do now, CD?’

‘I guess we need a bit of time. Why don’t we send them all off field-walking with the TV crew, then the three of us can have a think.’

That was what they did. The diggers went off across the hilltop in a long straggling line, searching for artefacts and signs of further human habitation. Maxwell accumulated a pocketful of oddly shaped stones. Gaye broke the buckle on her shoe. Aidan saved the day by finding a Tudor coin which had nothing at all to do with their dig but distracted everybody nicely. It bought enough time for Dozer, working with infinite care, to expose the eggshell fragments of a tiny human skull. They covered the skeleton as the diggers came back.

HESCROFT ARRIVED LATER and he, Camden and Patrick sat in the catering tent, while Bobby buttered bread.

Hescroft had the closed look he usually wore when money was at issue. ‘We’re faced with a tough decision, I fear, about where we go from here. Patrick, first of all, I should tell you that Kenny has made a suggestion about funding the rest of the dig which requires us to make a fairly substantial contribution to costs. Now, that it isn't the sort of thing we usually do. We would perhaps have hoped that the television side of it might have covered a higher proportion of the total.' He looked at Kenny Camden, who was lighting a cigarette.

'Unfortunately—' Camden began.

'Unfortunately, you'll have to put that out,' said Bobby from behind him. 'This is a food preparation area.'

'I'm afraid she's right,' said Patrick.

Camden bent down reluctantly to stub it out in the grass.

'Could you give us a few minutes?' said Hescroft to Bobby.

'Not if you want lunch on time,' said Bobby.

'We have to discuss delicate matters.'

'Your choice. Go outside and I won't hear you. Stay inside and I'll try not to listen.'

They stayed inside.

'As I was saying,' said Camden, 'the reaction I'm getting, unfortunately, is that there isn't anything very earth-shattering about an Anglo-Saxon burial. You know very well how much TV archaeology there is these days. There's bone shows everywhere. It's in danger of being done to death. We're looking for something new. Personalities. Now you've got Dozer and CD, and they're both good on camera, but it's not enough to make anyone sit up and take notice, so there's a limit on what we can risk at this stage.'

'Well, I'm afraid I don't think my company can afford to fill the gap,' said Hescroft. 'It's a shame really.'

This is a set-up, Patrick thought with sudden certainty. 'I suppose it would be different if you could do the ex-rock star angle,' he said innocently.

Camden, who had been staring at the ground in the pose of someone who was reluctantly heading for a tough decision, lifted his head a little too sharply.

'Well, yes,' he said, 'it certainly would, but I thought that wasn't really an option.'

'It's not,' said Patrick, his suspicions confirmed.

'I don't know there's a lot else that can save it,' said Hescroft a little too eagerly. 'What a pity.'

'I have considered other angles,' said Camden.

Oh yes, I'm sure you have, thought Patrick. 'Such as?' he said.

Camden was clearly scratching around. 'Well, there's this strange business of the song,' he said.

'What song?' asked Hescroft.

'This guy, this old farm bloke, sings in the pub,' said Camden. 'He sang this song about a woman who was supposed to be buried up here. That's how your friend Patrick here found this grave. Didn't you know?'

'Is that right?' said Hescroft to Patrick, bewildered.

'Up to a point.' He looked at Camden. 'I didn't know you'd heard about it.'

'It doesn't work, though,' said Camden, 'not in TV terms.'

'You didn't tell me,' said Hescroft, glaring at Patrick. 'You could have had us all on a complete wild-goose chase. Have you any idea how much this sort of thing costs?'

Virtually nothing, the way you do it, thought Patrick. He felt like a poker player holding all four aces. 'The song by itself wouldn't have made me want to dig,' he said. 'Finding the bead convinced me.'

'Just as well,' said Camden, 'considering the song was about a woman. What you've got here is a man, after all.'

'Well, no,' said Patrick. 'It's not.'

Everything was suddenly completely clear. They were trying to present him with stark alternatives. Insist on privacy and have the dig cancelled, or agree to be ex-star Paddy Kane playing at archaeology and carry on. He decided to play his ace in the hole, the third option.

'It's not a man. It's a woman.'

Bobby gasped and Hescroft made a tutting sound. 'Come off it. How could you possibly know that for certain?' He held up a hand. 'I know what you're going to say. The shape of the skull, right? No pronounced brow ridges? Rounded upper margin to the orbit? It never gives you a definite answer. For God's sake, Patrick, there are no female Anglo-Saxon burials with weapons. It's adult males only.'

'I'm not going by her skeleton at all,' said Patrick. 'I'm going by someone else's skeleton.'

Hescroft made a derisive noise. 'How can someone else's skeleton tell you anything at all about this one?'

'It's the bones of her baby. She was pregnant.'

Bobby dropped the bowl of lettuce she was holding.

'A pregnant warrior woman?' said Camden. 'All right. Now we've got a show.'

'That's extraordinary,' said Hescroft. 'We'd better have a look.'

'We haven't told the diggers yet.'

'Why don't you tell them now?' said Camden. 'We'll shoot it.'

Patrick let them leave the tent first then turned to share the moment with Bobby—a brief, jubilant conspiracy.

They took the grave cover off and the diggers, realising something was in the air, gathered round. Hescroft knelt in the earth in his smart linen trousers and stared at the bones.

'No doubt about it,' he murmured. 'Absolutely extraordinary.'

Jack set up the camera and Patrick, forgetting entirely that it was there, told all of them what it was they had found, and for the first time his words came out with fire. When he finished, they all stood staring at the tiny skeleton in sombre silence.

The questions came that night when the TV men had gone.

'Is everyone here?' said Patrick, as they sat around the campfire.

'Gaye isn't,' said Dozer.

'Yes, I am,' she said, stepping into the firelight. 'Sorry, I dropped my lipstick down the loo.'

'Did you get it back?' asked Dozer.

'I decided no one needs lipstick *that* much,' she said primly.

'Blimey, Gaye, you're going native,' he said, and she joined in the roar of laughter.

CD lay back on the grass, staring at the first stars. 'I hope you guys all realise,' he said, 'that you've lucked in to a dig that's going to be in all the textbooks.'

'Facts first,' said Patrick. 'One female pregnant skeleton, with a shield across her chest. Plus, about six foot from the feet of the skeleton, Gaye has uncovered what looks like a section of a very good sword blade. The metal must have been fantastic. It hasn't all corroded away.'

'Nitrides,' said the American. 'Remember, it's the chicken blade.'

Patrick looked at him sharply.

'Joe sang it. That's good enough for me,' said CD. 'I believe it. In the evenings, anyway. Daytime, I turn back into a scientist.'

'Leaving that aside for the moment, there's what looks like the remains of a chatelaine.'

'Which is what exactly?' asked Aidan.

'It's usually a ring or a brooch that's also a sort of a toilet kit, with things hanging on it like tweezers and little picks.'

'The significance,' CD added, 'is that chatelaines only come with females, if anyone was still in any doubt.'

'Don't you find yourself wondering what she was called?' said Gaye. 'I'd really like to know.'

Everyone knew what she meant and that was the moment at which the woman in the grave started to become in their minds something much more than an assembly of old bones.

'So, we have an enormous question to answer,' said Patrick. 'Everything we know about the period tells us they were very hierarchical. Men fought, women didn't. The oldest son got the father's weapons.'

'The oldest son was dead,' said Bobby, 'so were the others. The song said so.'

'I don't remember anything about the oldest son?'

'Joe sang it in the pub, the first time,' said Aidan.

'Can you remember it?'

'I can,' said Bobby. 'There are one or two verses I know.'

She spoke them with a lilt that set the tune humming in their heads.

'They met the raiders, blade to blade
In a spray of blood by the old stockade.
Outnumbered by them five to one,
The fight was led by the oldest son.

At the moment when they saw him fall,
And his soul took flight to the warriors' hall,
The hills rang out to a chilling cry.
Their father saw the young prince die.

He burst on them, this vengeful lord
And he whirled the blade of the chicken sword.
They fell at his feet like stalks of corn
Harvested for his dear first-born.'

'We've got to avoid putting too much faith in the song,' said Patrick. 'What we do here is going to be under close scrutiny. If it appears that we're being led by the song we'll just look stupid.'

Bobby backed him up. 'My father taught Joe the song and I expect he got it from his father, I don't know for sure.'

'Surely,' said Aidan, 'he couldn't be singing it word for word the way he heard it. No one could do that.'

'I'm not so sure,' said Bobby. 'Joe's got an amazing memory and I sometimes hear him practising in his room. It's the only time I ever hear his voice in the house.'

Patrick caught a glimpse of how lonely life must be for her. 'I wish I'd listened more closely,' he said. 'What else have we missed?'

'I know a few more bits of it,' said Bobby. 'She tries to save her people from these raiders and they kill her brothers and then, in the end, she's killed too.'

'What surprises me,' said Mary, the woman with the huge trowel, who normally kept herself to herself, 'is that a woman would fight. She'd have been better off running away.'

'You don't know that. You have to hold your ground sometimes,' said Bobby. 'Haven't you ever felt angry enough to attack a man?'

'Oh no, I don't think I have,' said Mary rather primly.

'Well, I have,' said Gaye, looking meaningfully at Dozer.

'I would have picked up a sword if I'd had to,' Bobby went on. 'If someone threatened the people I loved. So would lots of women. You're not trying to tell me that wasn't true in those days too? Peter, what do you think?'

'Well, there's the precedent of Boudicca, Queen of the Iceni, an East Anglian tribe. She led a rebellion against the Romans in AD 60.'

'If she could take up arms and be that sort of queen, so could our lady here,' said Bobby.

'Maybe.' Peter sounded cautious. 'But Boudicca was a Celt. The Saxons seem to have been more male-dominated.'

The talk moved in circles until one o'clock, then a sharp chill descended and drove them to their tents.

Patrick couldn't sleep, and after half an hour he got up and took a torch over to the burial site. The sky was on fire with stars. He paused for a while outside the frame tent protecting the grave, then opened the zip. The woman showed white in the torchlight and he knelt beside the trench and stared at her. Only a week ago he had stood beside a grave in a Welsh churchyard.

David's bones would be more substantial than this never-to-be-born Saxon child but that was all David was now, just bones and a tear-pricking memory.

SEVEN

The waning moon showed Patrick his escape route from the open grave. He stumbled across the rough hilltop, seeing in his mind's eye the well-worn movie of the funeral. Rachel's father came at him yet again, yelling accusations through that frozen crowd of mourners. He saw one hand reach out for his neck and the other, clenched, pulling back for the blow. Eyes tight shut, he stopped to take sucking, sobbing breaths of air.

Then he heard footsteps.

Patrick opened his eyes. Out of the darkness, a man was coming for him, a real man in the same space that the memory of Rachel's father had occupied, rushing at him in the same way so that Patrick recoiled, horrified, yelled and put his arm across his face to ward off the blow.

No blow came this time. Joe stared at him with profound sorrow on his face. He looked into Patrick's eyes, then reached out a tentative hand and touched him with flat, coarse fingers on the centre of his forehead. It felt to Patrick like something you might do to a frightened animal, and it eased his breathing as Joe walked rapidly away down the track towards the farmhouse.

Patrick shivered and the memory of the funeral came back to claim him again. Rachel's father's punches hadn't hurt nearly as much as his words of denunciation. Patrick hadn't tried to defend himself. After the assault he had lain still on the ground. Not one person from Rachel's tribe stepped forward to help him to his feet. Patrick's cousins, the only members of his own meagre family present, faded away, too, and he was left to slink away out of their lives.

Again there were real footsteps in the Oxfordshire night. This time Bobby coalesced out of the blackness, running up the track towards him.

'Patrick? Joe woke me. He was worried. I could tell. What's wrong?'

He tried to drive her away with the brutal truth.

'I'm here because I'm not a nice man. Because that grave up there has made me remember something I did that no nice man would ever have done, OK? Do you want to hear about it?' He heard no reply. 'Do you?' he insisted savagely. 'Because if you don't, then go home.'

In the moonlight he saw her nod. Just as Joe could sing to his depersonalised pub audience, so Patrick found he could speak to this listener to whom the moon gave a third face, not the Rachel-face, nor the candlelit madonna, but something else, something inscrutable.

'I was on stage in Rome,' he said. 'It was part of the Debt Relief concert, all that African starvation stuff. Worldwide TV coverage. Do you know "Wedding Vows"? My very own bloody awful song?'

'Yes, I know it,' she said. 'I've heard it. Everybody's heard it.'

'Well, I wasn't going to sing it. I hated it before it was even released. But that night I'd had a bottle of tequila and God knows what else, and the organisers came in to say they didn't want it. Not in the spirit of the concert.'

'You sang it anyway?'

'Yes, I sang it but that wasn't the point. I dedicated it live to my wife Rachel. Live, in front of two hundred million people. I wasn't even supposed to have a wife. And I said I meant every single word of it.' He stared at her face, still impassive in the moon-gleam. 'I'm not a nice man.'

'What happened afterwards?' said Bobby. 'She left you, didn't she?'

'Oh, come on. You must know. You've been looking me up.'

'Not since I told you. You don't like people prying, do you? So I haven't pried. You can't have it both ways. Don't complain that I don't know.'

It was a moment when Patrick might very easily have poured it all out. He wanted to do just that. Then, standing on the edge of that vertiginous slope, knowing that to move even one more step meant demolishing the buttressing walls protecting him from the world, Patrick pulled back.

'I lost her,' he said. 'That's all.'

In the silence that followed, Bobby turned the silver mirror of her face slightly away. 'I don't mean this cruelly,' she said eventually, 'but you're not the only one. I've lost someone—a partner. I do speak that language.'

How could she say that, he thought with fury. She didn't even know what he was talking about. He meant death, not separation.

'A *partner*?' he said. 'I'm not talking about a partner. You can lose a partner. You can find another one. It just takes time. There are far worse things than that. There are things you can't replace.'

He might as well have slapped her, the way the impact of his words knocked her head back.

'I came here to try to help you,' she said. 'My mistake, maybe, but you can't bully me into thinking you're as bad as you say you are. I'll make up my own mind. I'm going back home because I don't think there's anything else useful I can say right now.'

She walked away, leaving him in his self-inflicted hell.

IT WAS THE MORNING after the concert, the morning after his brutal dedication. They were on the road again, leaving Rome, the phones in the tour bus ringing nonstop. Every rock journalist and gossip columnist in Britain was after the story of Paddy Kane's unsuspected little wife back home. The press were out for blood and plenty was promised by the way Paddy had revealed and reviled Rachel in the same instant. Every PR person on Colonic Music's payroll was frantically trying to put the genie back in the bottle.

The bus stopped for a lunch break in the ancient city of Perugia. There Paddy saw the boy playing in the bright spangles of light. When he came out and Claypole told him Rachel and David were both dead, it didn't seem, for a moment, that it could possibly be true.

He heard Claypole tell the outlines of what he knew. Rachel had never even made it down the drive of their house. Her car had hit the wall on the bend of the drive and ricocheted into the river. David was found drowned in the back seat next to an open bag, messily stuffed with the few things she had grabbed before rushing out of the house. Nobody knew exactly when it had happened.

Paddy knew. Paddy knew it had been within minutes of his song going out across the world's ether. He had run back into the cathedral, had walked blindly into a side chapel, the full, dreadful pity of it all crystallising in his head into a sharper and sharper pain, showing him that below all the surface scum of the past years he still loved Rachel. Far more acutely, he knew he loved David with his whole soul and that the future he had created held agony and guilt in huge and equal measure.

In the side chapel he saw an immense carved crucifix towering over him, dark and threatening. He turned his eyes quickly away and found himself looking up to where light burst through a stained-glass semicircle. The image in the glass was a wild, white-haired God in yellow robes whose eyes tore right through him and whose arm stretched down to point an accusing finger directly at him.

The band and its manager never saw Paddy Kane again.

After the funeral, Patrick had come to understand the full extent of what he had made Rachel suffer, but it was David's voice he would hear in the middle of the night, time and time again.

Now, before he went to sleep in his tent, Patrick wrote a note to Bobby and left it beside the gas ring. It just said, 'Thank you. I shouldn't have said that.'

Then he climbed into his sleeping-bag, looking out at the square shape covering the grave, trying to convince himself it was not his own past they had disturbed under the earth.

IT WAS HOT THE NEXT MORNING and what had been packed, moist earth deep below the topsoil had now dried out except in the patch of clay where Gaye had been digging. Dozer's shirt was damp with sweat across his back. He raised an eyebrow when Patrick came towards him, holding his trowel.

'Hello,' he said, 'funny how directors only get their 'ands dirty when you start finding the good stuff.'

‘I’m going to give Gaye a hand with the sword,’ Patrick said. He needed to lose himself in the painstaking work of digging. He needed distraction because David had come to him in the night, as he always did when Patrick let the memories out of their tight box. David, forever four years old, with Rachel’s huge eyes in a face that was otherwise entirely Patrick’s, had stood over him, soaking wet, and skipped back beyond his reach whenever he tried to touch him.

Patrick had woken searching for David, to find instead Bobby’s disembodied arm, reaching in through the tent’s door, offering a mug of coffee.

‘Did you see my note?’ he’d asked.

‘That’s why you get the coffee. One of the reasons, anyway.’

‘I shouldn’t have said any of that.’

‘If you ask me, you should have said more.’

‘Well, I shouldn’t have said it like that.’

‘No argument there. Anyway, there’s a deputation to see you. The vicar and the head teacher. If you don’t come soon I may have to take up Dozer’s offer and hire his mate, the fancy cake chef.’

‘The vicar? Where are they?’

‘Sniffing around by the grave. On my land. Without asking.’

PULLING ON HIS CLOTHES, Patrick shot out into the sunlight and found the Reverend Augustus Templeton-Jones trying to undo the zip of the tent that protected the grave. A man in tweeds was standing behind him, the man Patrick had seen fending off Bobby at their first brief meeting.

‘Leave that alone, please,’ he called, irritated. ‘That’s a protected environment.’ It sounded good and it stopped the vicar in his tracks.

‘I do beg your pardon,’ he said. He was bald on top with white side whiskers, and he didn’t look sorry at all. In daylight, Patrick could see he had a sharply hooked nose that swept down in an unbroken curve from his forehead. The headmaster stood back, embarrassed.

‘What can I do for you?’

‘Word has reached me,’ said the vicar, ‘that you have made a further find. A crucifix, I believe. Is it true?’

'A crucifix? No, I'm afraid not.'

'Well, I apologise if I have been misinformed, but I understood that you had found a brooch in that form.'

'Look, the only brooch we have found is bent, broken and badly damaged. As far as we can see it's got three arms but—'

'If one arm was missing, that would make four. Four arms is a crucifix, young man.'

'At the moment, it's a broken brooch, that's all. Three arms. Ask me again in a month when it's been cleaned.'

'I also wanted to talk to you about another matter.' The vicar looked towards the tents. 'The woman who is doing your cooking, Miss Redhead.'

'What about her?'

'Just a word of warning. I understand that many people in this village have had problems with her attitude since her return. I'm afraid to say she has a reputation for causing trouble.'

Her return? Patrick wondered what he meant by that but didn't want to discuss Bobby any more than he had to.

The head teacher broke his silence and his voice was peevish. 'As a case in point she is currently trying to get what you might call a civil disobedience campaign started among the parents in the village.'

'You're talking about the May Day parade? I don't quite understand your objection to it.'

The vicar stepped in quickly. 'It teaches the children a form of idolatry, Mr Kane. In effect they worship a graven image. Miss Redhead attempts to justify it in the name of tradition but this has every sign of a recent invention. It is directly against everything the Bible teaches us.'

'I thought Green Man images are found in carvings in quite a lot of churches?'

'Neglect of proper forms by long-dead wood carvers is greatly to be regretted. May I urge you to have as little to do with her as possible?'

'She is a valuable member of our team.'

'You will see the error of your ways.'

'That's quite right,' piped up the other man, 'you will. Good day to you.'

THE EXPOSED SECTION of the sword blade was six inches long and, brushing at the surface with a stiff paintbrush, Patrick was amazed at the condition. It was an even mid-brown colour, with nothing more than small surface irregularities caused by what seemed to be corrosion. He brushed harder and all at once could see regular markings.

'CD,' he called, 'you're the sword expert. Come and look at this.'

'What have you found, chicken feathers?'

'Patterning, maybe.'

CD took a large magnifying glass from one of the many zip pockets of his bulging waistcoat and stared at the blade for a long time in silence. Then he got to his feet as Patrick spoke.

'What do you think?'

'You were hoping this was pattern-welded, right?' said CD.

'Maybe.'

'What's pattern-welding?' said Aidan from the other trench.

'Get back to work, you son of a dog,' said CD. 'This is not for your ears.'

'Why not?' said Patrick. 'It's about time for another sword lecture. Especially when there's a real sword to talk about.'

CD gave him an inscrutable look. 'You may regret that,' he said. 'You may also want to leave off uncovering much more until dear Kenny and his merry men are here . . . well, his merry man anyway.' He bellowed at the others. 'All right, leave your trowels and come and soak up some wisdom, folks.'

The shout reached Bobby in the catering tent. Patrick saw her come out into the sunshine and stride towards them and he realised how glad he was that she didn't seem to bear grudges. He turned his gaze quickly back to CD.

'The boss here wants me to tell you all about pattern-welding,' said CD. 'Pattern-welding in sword blades produces interesting curvy herringbone sort of effects in the metal. Mostly it came from the way they put the blades together to get the right strength. Now, for our current state of knowledge, we are indebted to a man named Anstee, who didn't believe all the complicated theoretical garbage the sword experts were writing so he went and made one himself. He twisted together different bits of iron, a sort of club sandwich of flat strips and square bars and then he—'

'Fed them to the chickens?' suggested Maxwell.

'Well now, smarty-pants,' said CD, 'no, he didn't, *but* he did heat them up in a special paste, which if I recall rightly was made up of honey, flour, olive oil, milk and . . . guess what.'

'Ostrich droppings, chicken poo, elephant dung?'

'No, no, no. Pigeon shit,' said CD triumphantly. 'Anyway to cut a long story short, Anstee forged it all together and, lo and behold, he'd made a beautiful patterned sword.'

'And that's what we've got here, is it?' said Aidan.

'No,' said CD, 'I'm afraid not.'

'So why have you been telling us all about it?' said Aidan.

'I was asked to talk about pattern-welded sword blades.'

'But this isn't one?' said Patrick. 'I thought I saw a pattern.'

'Maybe you did,' said CD, smiling in delight.

'Well, how do you know it isn't pattern-welding?'

'Because when you try to weld wood, all it does is catch fire.'

'Wood? It looks like rusty iron.'

'I grant you that, but it's not. It's wood. Fragile as hell now but very hard once. I guess it's only there at all thanks to that spring.'

'Why's that?' said Aidan.

'Anaerobic conditions. No oxygen. That means the organisms that would normally destroy the wood can't survive. We'll have to be very, very careful because this is special. We've got to keep it wet.'

'Why's it so special? If it isn't a sword, what is it?'

'Did I say it wasn't a sword? Did I?'

There were scattered replies of 'No' and 'You didn't', except from Dozer who said, 'I can never understand a bloody word you say anyway.'

'My guess is it's a sword all right, but it's a little wooden one, kinda like a half-scale model,' CD went on.

'What use is a wooden sword?'

'You thought you could see a pattern,' said CD to Patrick.

'Yes. What was it? The grain?'

'Some of it, sure. But the rest is much, much better.' CD proffered his magnifying glass. 'Runes. I can see two of them pretty clearly and I'll make a prediction.' He turned to look at the others. 'Important professional waiver here, guys and gals. Archaeologists don't make predictions because it's always too early . . .' he paused expectantly.

'. . . to tell,' they replied as one.

'Notwithstanding that,' he said, '—by the way, do you dig the truly English polysyllables?—notwithstanding that, I predict that when we uncover the rest of this, one end will be burnt. The only other wooden sword like this one I've come across—and if anyone's interested I do have copies of the appendix to my second doctoral thesis available at just nine dollars and ninety-nine cents—had a runic inscription that ran something like "return messenger", which fits the fact that it was burnt.'

Patrick remembered. 'Burnt arrows were a summons for help. It meant someone was in extreme danger. The other wooden sword came from Germany, didn't it?'

'Frisia,' said CD, 'on the coast.' He waved vaguely. 'Holland, is it? Dutchland, Deutschland, what's the difference?'

'There speaks a citizen of the country that was too busy to join in the first half of the big match,' said Dozer, sourly.

'Ah, come on, Doze,' said CD. 'We're all Germans really if you go back far enough.'

Patrick took the magnifier and knelt over the exposed part of the sword. It was drying out fast, to reveal a worm trail of lighter-coloured earth, embedded in the grooves. He made out a vertical line, with two parallel diagonals sloping down from its right—the 'æ' rune of Old English. The other shape eluded him. He couldn't be sure if it was the M shape that spelt 'e' or had the two extra lines of the 'd' rune.

'So what's with these runes anyway?' asked Maxwell, but suddenly there was a good reason to hurry.

'We'll talk about that this evening,' said Patrick. 'This is an amazing find and we need to protect it. It's out in the open air now and that's the worst possible thing.'

'Cover it up again,' said CD, and Patrick scooped wet clay from each side of the exposed wood, patting it into place over the sword to seal it from the air. Patrick called Hescroft and a conservation specialist from the Pitt-Rivers Museum in Oxford was on her way to them in minutes.

Hescroft also alerted the TV crew so the rest of Patrick's day was taken up satisfying them as much as superintending the painstaking removal of the wooden sword. When the last of the soil was carefully removed from the sword's pointed tip the black marks of old scorching were clear to see.

The specialist was a forthright Danish woman.

'Get that camera out of the way,' she snapped. 'You shouldn't have left it uncovered *at all*. Do you know how fragile this is? There is no time to lose. Bloody archaeologists.'

'So what do we do?'

'You do nothing. You stand still and watch. I take it out as a block. Slice down and under it, three inches at least below it so we support it from under and lift it like that.'

She did it under their anxious eyes, sliding a thin sheet of plywood beneath it. When it was safely on the grass, she wrapped the entire block tightly in clingwrap.

'I take it back now for proper treatment,' she said. 'Soak it in polyethylene glycol. Wax soluble in water. Gives it strength, or maybe I'll freeze-dry it. We'll see about that.'

When she'd gone and the camera had left them alone, Patrick found himself standing next to an unexpectedly thoughtful CD.

'What is it?' Patrick asked.

CD shrugged and Edgar, perched on his shoulder, fluttered indignantly. 'Hard to say. First he was a he, then she was a she, with a little one. Now there's this. Her distress call. I guess she's not just bones any more.'

'What do you make of the sword? Did she send it? Did she get it from someone else?'

'Speculation,' said CD. 'I only speculate after sundown.'

'It's six o'clock,' said Patrick.

'Sundown's a-comin',' said CD squinting at the sky. 'Just another couple of hours to get the Glenboggy in.'

'My turn,' said Patrick.

Patrick got in his car and drove down to the Stag. As he slowed down to turn into the pub car park, he noticed a little knot of people on the village green and saw with surprise that Kenny Camden and Jack were there with the camera. They seemed to be interviewing a group of people. He parked the car and walked over. Camden didn't see Patrick coming up behind him.

'So you agree with the vicar?' Camden said. 'If the woman does turn out to be Christian, you think she should be decently reburied?'

'Well, I do,' said a large woman. 'That would be the decent thing.'

Patrick cleared his throat loudly and Camden swung round.

'A word in your ear,' said Patrick coldly.

'I won't be a minute,' said Camden to the group, and glanced at Jack, nodding slightly. Patrick led him into the centre of the triangular green, aware that the whole group was staring after them.

'Who said you could do this?' he demanded. 'I had an earful from the vicar this morning. I wondered how he knew about the brooch. I didn't realise you were going around egging everybody on.'

'I've got a programme to make,' said Camden. 'I don't tell you about archaeology, you don't tell me about TV, OK?'

'No, not OK at all. We've got the security of the site to think about. You're prejudicing the whole dig.'

'To be frank, I think you're being a bit precious, Paddy.'

'Do *not* call me Paddy. I've told you enough times.'

'Oh, come off it,' said Camden to goad him. 'Big deal—Paddy, Pat, so what? I can't help it. It's the way I think of you.'

Patrick's fingers clenched into a fist and he fought to get back under control. 'Yes, that's the whole trouble. Time you stopped. I understand you have a job to do but you don't have to do it this way. I'm not here to be used and I'm pissed off with this. I'll do the job, but leave me alone, understand?'

'Understood,' said Camden soothingly. 'We'll stay out of your hair if you just play ball a little.'

As Patrick stalked across to the pub, Camden strolled back to Jack and the camera. 'You did get that, didn't you?' he said.

'Yes,' said Jack, rather regretting that he had. 'You won't hear much of it because I couldn't get that close but you'll see all the arm-waving and that. He was pretty worked up.'

'That's my boy,' said Camden.

SUPPER WAS STEW ON PASTA, though Bobby called it tagliatelle giardiniera. It didn't matter. Six litres of the Stag's cheapest red wine chased the taste away, and it seemed the diggers could hardly wait for darkness and the campfire chat.

'Do you think Joe's coming tonight?' Dozer asked Bobby.

'He's here already,' she said, nodding into the gloom, and there was her brother, standing motionless on the fringe of the firelight.

'No gitbox?' said Dozer.

'What?'

'As his official translator,' said CD, 'I can reveal that what appeared to be a random series of unintelligible grunts actually meant "The man in question has not come bearing his stringed instrument for making mellifluous music, namely his guitar."'

'Come and join us, mate,' called Dozer, but there was no sign Joe had even heard.

'He'll come if he wants to,' said Bobby.

'No songs tonight, then,' Gaye said.

'Who knows?' Bobby said, smiling.

'So what do we think?' said Patrick, when they'd all settled down round the fire. 'It's after sundown, CD, and your jackdaw's tucked up. You're allowed to speculate now.'

'Raven,' said the American. 'All in good time. Let's lay out the facts. We have a pregnant Anglo-Saxon woman, probably seventh century, buried with a shield, and close by we have a half-size wooden sword burnt at one end and inscribed with runes. Both of these are very, very, very unusual. She is also accompanied by grave goods typical of female burials, plus we now think there is a real metal sword in the grave beside the skeleton.'

'We do?' said Patrick, startled.

'Sorry, forgot to tell you. It's too early, et cetera. Just a sign of something blade-like so far. While you were fetching the booze. Speaking of which, you seem to be clutching a bottle under your arm which I have not yet been introduced to.'

'It's Teacher's. They didn't have any rotgut.'

'I'll manage. So, speculate away, folks.'

'I bet she sent the sword for help at the last minute,' Gaye said, 'and they didn't come in time so she had to defend her children herself. Then when they did come, it was too late, so they buried the sword with her.'

'You think she had other children?' Maxwell was curious.

'Of course she did,' said Gaye. 'If she was pregnant she would have run and hid. Anything to defend her unborn baby. She would only have fought if she had other children to protect.'

'Is that right?'

'I think it is,' said Bobby. 'I've seen that.'

'Where?' said Patrick, surprised.

'Oh . . . that's a sidetrack.'

She was looking into the fire. Feeling his gaze on her, she glanced sideways at him, making a little face as if to dismiss the remark.

That he had been staring at the silhouette of her face for far too long was not noticed, because something else had grabbed everybody's attention. Joe was coming to join them round their fire.

He sat down on a log between Aidan and Gaye, looking at each of them in turn, meeting their eyes. There was a moment of silence then, holding out the whisky bottle, CD said, 'Nice to see you, pal. We'd been hoping you'd join us.'

Joe, dressed in a green army-surplus sweater and patched cord trousers, took the bottle, lifted it to his lips and passed it on. Patrick could see no trace of a family resemblance to Bobby. Her brother had a square, weather-beaten face, his grey hair was short and curly, and under bushy eyebrows his bright, pale eyes darted from side to side.

As they stared at him, he took a breath and sang three descending notes softly, 'Ah, ah, ah.' Then he looked at them enquiringly and sang the same three notes again. He stood up and held out both hands, palms up, in front of him, nodding at them.

Bobby sang the notes back at him, accurately, and he beamed with pleasure.

'Our turn, folks,' said Bobby. 'He wants us to sing the notes.'

It was ragged at first and Joe kept signing for them to start again. After five false starts, they sounded reasonably good. At that point, Joe made a chopping, cut-off sign with his hand and held up two fingers. This time he sang six notes, starting low and soaring up only to descend again. They'd got the idea now and it only took three tries to get it right. He confused them briefly by holding up one finger, but Bobby said it meant they should do the first one again and he nodded, beaming. One finger for the first, two fingers for the second. They did them one after the other until he was satisfied, then he held up three fingers.

'Blimey, how much more is there?' said Dozer. 'If we're doing Handel's *Messiah* in bite-size chunks, we're going to be here all night.'

They learned the third and fourth sections quickly. Then Joe beckoned them all to their feet with upward sweeps of his arms.

'I guess it's show time,' said CD, echoing Patrick's thoughts.

Joe walked off into the darkness and they followed as he led them up the gentle slope of the hilltop. They stopped in front of the frame tent protecting the woman and her child, and Joe went to it, holding one corner pole and looking towards Patrick.

'You want us to move it?' Patrick asked, and he saw Joe give another of his sharp downward nods. 'OK,' he said. 'Give us a hand to get the pegs out,' and the diggers moved the big tent carefully so that the grave lay bare.

Joe took a step closer to the grave and knelt as if in prayer. Then he got back to his feet, turned to the group and held up a single finger. He hummed the first note for a moment as a guide, looked round to check they were all ready and brought his finger sweeping down.

There was no hanging back in their response. All day the grave had been cluttered with the jarring gadgets of modern times. Now the night had brought back simplicity and they were just fourteen living souls on a hilltop honouring the dead with an ancient tune. The last note ended and they looked to Joe for guidance.

In the silence he half sang, half chanted:

'The boda came to Abbandun at evening bell,
Brought by the child with sunset head.
We left our looms to answer it as black night fell,
That blood call on the summoning sword.'

An involuntary shiver ran through Patrick's body. Joe's pronunciation was precise and oddly foreign. 'Night' sounded almost like the German 'nicht' and 'blood' was 'bloode'. Intent on what he was doing, Joe held up a hand again and, carried along by the rhythm, they all knew that the second part followed. The notes they sang took on a beauty beyond anything they had sung before and, when it ended, Joe went on:

'The mother river broke its banks that heartless night
And slowed our feet in beds of mud
When we climbed to your shattered hall at dawn's first light
You'd taken ship on seas of blood.'

This time, they needed no prompting at all, coming in unison into the third part.

'Your husband's kin, who failed to pay the sword-blade debt
Now stand before you with bowed head.
We came too late to help in time of need and yet
We vow we'll keep your daughter fed.'

They all stood in stunned silence, Patrick staring up into the heavens. Those stars aren't really there at all, he thought, although I can see them. What I see is just a message from where they were a thousand years or a thousand millennia ago, from where they were when this woman was laid in the ground.

He pulled his gaze back to the earth. Joe was gone and the rest of them were looking at each other as if shocked by what they'd done. After a long moment, Patrick went over to the covering tent. CD and Dozer helped him walk it back into its place, then they all moved back to the fire and settled into their places around it.

CD produced the bottle of Scotch and it made the rounds. Then the American said, 'Before you ask, Aidan, Abbandun is the old Anglo-Saxon name for Abingdon, which is, I would say, four hours' hard march away in the times before there were roads.'

'Thank you,' said Aidan nodding. 'I hadn't yet thought of asking that. I *was* going to ask about the unfamiliar word there at the start. Sounded like boder.'

'It means nothing to me. Peter? No?'

'It was clear what the sense was,' said Maxwell, almost indignantly. 'The boder was the summons, wasn't it?'

CD shrugged. 'This is beyond my humble knowledge.'

Dozer nodded slowly. 'What gets me,' he said, 'is that I'm the king of the cynics but all the time I was listening to him, I was quite sure he wasn't just making it up.'

'It was special,' said Gaye. 'In fact, I think it was more . . . more wonderfully disturbing than anything else in my life. Last time the grave was open, they were laying her in it. I'd really like to think those words were more or less what they were saying then.'

That's quite a speech, thought Patrick, coming from Gaye who'd only seemed to feel strongly about hygiene when she first arrived.

'You can't say those were the same words, can you?' objected Maxwell. 'What he said tonight, that was modern English.'

'Oh, it's not so very different,' said Peter. 'The Old English words just got added to, a bit of French and a bit of Danish here and there. If you just take the time to learn to pronounce Old English, the mystery disappears. It wouldn't be hard to put together an Old English sentence that you'd understand with no trouble at all.'

'Boda, with an a,' said CD, who clearly hadn't been listening. 'Idiot. Maxwell, I owe you an apology. B, O, D, A—berkano, othila, dagaz, ansuz.'

'Bless you,' said Dozer, 'that's a nasty cold.'

'Names from the runic alphabet. I told you about the goddamn Frisian sword. That's half of what's written on it. The second word, boda. Wait. Do not move.' He leapt to his feet, ran to his tent and came back with a heavy book and a torch.

'Bedtime reading,' he said, 'and you get to give your pecs a work-out at the same time. Bosworth and Toller's *Anglo-Saxon Dictionary*. Boda, boda, boda, yup. Masculine noun, meaning "messenger, ambassador, herald", et cetera.'

'A summons to help,' said Maxwell. 'I told you.'

'So if the runes on *our* sword say boda, that would be pretty strong support for the song,' said Aidan.

'Runic characters,' said CD. 'Just to be really purist, runes were the sacred stones they were cut into. But yes, I guess it would.'

'What are these runes about anyway?' said Aidan. 'I thought that was comic-book stuff. Hobbits and wizards.'

'Ask Peter, the one-man database,' said CD. 'He knows everything.'

'An early system of lettering,' said Peter, chuckling, 'made up of straight lines, probably because the letters were incised into stone or wood and it's easier to do straight lines if you're using a knife. The alphabet is called the futhark, just like we say ABC, because that's what the first six letters spelt.' He turned to Aidan. 'Before you ask, I know futhark has seven letters, but the third one is a combined "th" sound. Runic words were used not for communication but for symbolic purposes,' he went on. 'You might put a name on a valuable object to label it as yours but more likely to give it a certain power. There were those poor Britons, used to Roman culture—history, poetry and plays—and in come these crude foreigners whose entire literary heritage adds up to a row of grunts carved on a rock. They have to wait another six hundred years before there's anything else worth reading.'

There was a scatter of appreciative laughter, then a silence.

Gaye said it for all of them. 'I don't really care where that song came from. It's true enough for me. That's a burial over there, not just a dig. She was as alive as we are, that woman. If Joe's songs are the best way to remember that, then that's good enough for me.'

There was a bit of whispering in the darkness then Maxwell went off to his tent and came back holding something behind him. Aidan encouraged him onwards but the boy was reluctant. In the end Aidan took the guitar Maxwell was carrying and came over to Patrick.

'Now, Mr Director,' he said, 'we have a favour to ask.'

Patrick looked at the guitar, appalled. 'What?'

'We know you have a fine voice, having heard it tonight, and we know you're an archaeologist through and through these days, which is all that matters. Some of us have the idea that you might also be rather good on one of these things and we wondered whether you might be persuaded to give it a shot, among friends. Just some tuneful old things that we'd all know. It would be a kindness.'

So, astonishing himself, Patrick reached out and took the instrument, feeling with a shock of familiarity the swell of it against his thigh. He suddenly realised, as his fingers touched the strings, how long it was since he had last played a guitar for pleasure. It was an old cheap acoustic with nylon strings and it was out of tune. He spent much longer than was strictly necessary getting it right. Then without thinking about it, he found a reggae beat and launched into 'Redemption Song'. He hadn't played anything plainly tuneful since before Nam Erewhon, but his subconscious brought the words and the chords back as if the years in between hadn't happened at all. When a log-falling leap of firelight made him look up, he saw a circle of underworld, flame-painted faces all looking at him.

'C'mon, Pat, give us something we can dance to,' called Dozer. 'Me and Gaye want to rock and roll.'

'I do *not*,' said Gaye.

Patrick did his best with 'Blue Suede Shoes'. Dozer got to his feet, trying to pull Gaye with him but she wouldn't, then Bobby smiled and jumped up and she and Dozer went into a dance as if they'd rehearsed it a hundred times. Patrick repeated the verses he could remember over and over again just to watch the two of them, until Dozer dropped exhausted and Bobby danced on.

He played her to a whirling finale and, not wanting her to stop, slowed into a song that came out of his subconscious. Only when some of them joined in, did he realise what it was he was playing. '*I'm a young man, growing up in the world . . .*'

He willed her to stop dancing before the chorus came: '*If you want to know, how she makes love, just look at the way she dances.*' Perhaps Bobby recognised the tune too because she sat down suddenly and, in the firelight, he realised that her cheeks were wet with tears. She turned her gaze away into the flames but after a while, knowing his gaze was on her, she stared straight back at him, her eyes still shining, then got up and walked off.

The rest were intent on him and few saw her go. He could do or say nothing to stop her, halfway through his song. He brought it to a premature halt at the end of the next verse and rested.

They clapped him and they wouldn't let him stop. By the time Patrick had been through all he could remember from Dire Straits to Dylan, exhaustion settled on them. He was happier than he'd been for as long as he could remember. As he handed the guitar back to Maxwell, the boy said, 'That was just great. Famous you, singing just for us,' and he didn't even mind that.

Before he crawled into his tent, he looked down the hill at a single light burning in a dormer window at the farm and wondered what had caused Bobby's sudden flight.

EIGHT

If there was a single moment that explained how Pat became Paddy it was that first time he went out on stage with the band when the darkness beyond the lights erupted with three thousand voices. In that moment of utter astonishment he found that he could play them like an instrument—a whirl of his arm doubled the volume, a flick of his head brought in the girls' screaming trebles. Fear disappeared and utter confidence in his mastery of this audience flooded through him. He had what they wanted and he played their hunger. They responded with ecstasy and total, uncritical adulation and Pat was washed away by it.

Now, waking to the unfamiliar tingle that the guitar strings had left in his fingertips, Patrick was back on that stage again for a moment and the future was not yet written. In the next second, the nylon-filtered green light brought him back to a hard today, and he felt another unguarded morning pang for David and Rachel. People had told him you got over it but he wasn't even sure you ever got used to it.

He steeled himself to crawl outside, then went to the marquee for breakfast. He felt raw and open. Last night Bobby had danced like an angel and he had watched like a slave. She's the cook, he told himself. I'm the director. I will go in and be polite and that will be it. She was busy frying eggs and hardly had time to look round when he said good morning. He took slices of bread and a scoop of marmalade, poured coffee and went outside to sit on the grass where CD and Dozer were already eating their food. It was a fine morning and, for the first time since they had arrived, there was no dew.

'Take a look at that,' said CD. 'They're early.' He was pointing with his knife to where Camden's car was coming into sight through the gate.

'Maybe we won't mention last night,' said Patrick.

'My thoughts exactly. You go and occupy them for a minute or two and I might just spread the word round the gang.'

'I'll go,' said Dozer.

'No, no,' said CD. 'We merely want to delay him, not frighten him to death.'

The Toyota's tailgate was open and Camden was standing bent over, busy with papers in the back compartment, when Patrick walked up. Jack was sorting through his camera gear on the bonnet.

'Good morning,' said Patrick. 'You're bright and early.'

He took Camden by surprise. The man stood up sharply, cracked his head on the roof, yelped and dropped the cardboard file he was holding. As Patrick went to pick it up for him, he found himself staring, transfixed by a photocopy that had slid out of the folder. It was a page from a tabloid newspaper. He stared at the old headline: MAD PADDY BROKE MY CAMERA SAYS OUR SNAPPER. Anger rose in him that Camden should have such a thing in his files.

He heard Kenny Camden say, 'Whoops.' Then he tore the sheet into small pieces, and stuffed them into his pocket.

'Before you start,' said Camden, 'I forgot that was still there.'

'Why was it there in the first place?'

'Because I was finding out about you. I did my research. That's what you have to do when you're putting a programme together. I didn't know all this would be so sensitive for you. OK?'

'What else have you got in there?' said Patrick, pointing at the folder. 'I want to see it.'

'No, come on. It's private stuff.' Camden glanced round at Jack, to see that the cameraman now had his gear ready and it seemed to be casually pointing in their direction. 'Look, Patrick, I know you've had a rough time but I don't really know why. Maybe if you just told me a bit more, I could avoid treading on your toes.'

'Or you could jump on them harder.'

Camden decided to go for it. 'I know you lost your family. Car crash, wasn't it? No one could blame you for that.'

'You know nothing,' said Patrick. 'Nothing at all, and stop bloody prying into my affairs.'

'Look, I can see that maybe it's tough for you here. A grave with a mother and child.'

'That is nothing to do with it,' said Patrick, stung by the fact that it had everything to do with it. 'You shoot your stuff but stay off that. This is just a dig, nothing more. I'm going to work now.'

'Whatever you say. We'll be down in a minute.'

Camden watched Patrick walk away. 'Did you get all that, Jack?'

'No.'

'What do you mean, no? Do you mean you missed it all?'

'I had no idea you wanted me to shoot that. Sounded private to me.'

'Get this, you dickhead. *Nothing* is private where he comes in, OK?'

THE DIGGERS, ENJOYING their usual leisurely start to the day, were spread around the grass outside the marquee when Patrick arrived.

'Come on,' he barked. 'Let's get on with it.'

'It's only twenty past eight,' said CD.

Patrick turned to him. 'If I say it's time to start, it's time to start.' The words were out of his mouth before he could stop them.

'Easy, boss,' said Dozer. 'What's the matter? Hurricane expected?'

'No, sorry, guys. I had a punch-up with Camden.' Patrick made a big effort to smile and cancel out what he'd said, but it wasn't a complete success.

The diggers worked in a baffled silence until the day's first find gave them a common interest again.

'Take a look at *this*,' said CD.

Four small coins lay next to the woman's shoulder blade.

Though CD hadn't raised his voice at all, the antennae of the other diggers had started twitching and the usual ring quickly formed round the grave trench. Jack arrived with the camera.

Maxwell beat Aidan to the question. 'What are they?'

'Itett,' said CD.

'What's that?'

'Short for "it's too early to tell". But they could be sceattas, maybe?' The word sounded like 'shatters'.

'What are *they*?'

'Saxon silver coins,' said Peter promptly, 'usually cast in clay moulds, then stamped. But I'd say it's a bit early for them. Until the eighth century they're usually only found to the southeast of here.'

'Do you promise that you're not going to suddenly turn out to be somebody I should have heard of?' CD asked him.

'I'm afraid not,' said Peter smiling. 'I *am* a bit of a coin specialist, though.'

'So what else might they be?' said Maxwell.

Peter bent to pick one of them up but stopped himself in time and turned to CD. 'May I?'

'Give me a minute to get it on the record sheet. Couple of photos.' CD busied himself with the camera and the paperwork, then he gently loosened the top coin. 'OK, here you go.'

Peter rubbed at the surface. 'It's been pierced,' he said. 'There's a small hole near the rim. May I borrow your magnifying glass?'

CD passed it over and the older man inspected the coin carefully.

'All right,' he said. 'It's one of the type called radiates. Do you see there? There's a crown that radiates round the emperor's head? Looks like an antonianus to me. These coins are Roman. They could be as old as the third century.'

'So what are they doing here?'

'My guess is someone made them into a necklace. Look at the holes. You sometimes see them as pendants.'

'Well, dear lady,' said CD, looking down at the bones. 'Full of surprises ain't you? You just love those old Roman things.' He turned back to the others. 'You realise maybe we're looking at the first archaeologist here, folks? Hell, this stuff was three, four hundred years old when she was born. That's like me digging up a coin from the Stuarts. Pretty damned exciting, I'd call that.'

In the afternoon, Dozer found two pieces of shaped bone which he pronounced to be gaming counters. He went on trowelling away, and later exposed a flat slate. Wiping off the dirt, he discovered the incised straight lines of a superb gaming board. That stopped everything for quite some time, Kenny Camden wanting to know what the game was and even Peter not having an answer.

They were into the bottom four or five inches of the grave now, and the finds were coming thick and fast.

'Hey, look what's here. I think I've struck iron,' said CD.

In the next few minutes he uncovered several heavily rusted iron cleats, oblong plates in pairs, with the remains of rivets at each end holding them apart.

'It's the bed,' said Patrick. 'Her wooden bed. Just like in the song. There were cleats like that at Swallowcliffe. They held the planks together. And look, there's an eyelet. Cords went through those and held up a latticework support for the mattress.'

'"She lies there still on her wooden bed",' said CD. 'Oh, hi, Jack.'

Patrick whirled round and saw the cameraman with dismay. Jack, noticing that Camden was nowhere in the immediate vicinity, put a finger to his lips and winked.

The American uncovered more and more of the fragile remains of the bed, but it was Dozer who exclaimed next. 'I've found glass!' That brought the crowd round.

'Can you get it out quite quickly?' said Camden, reappearing. 'I've got to be in Oxford for a budget meeting at five.'

'No, he can't,' said Patrick shortly. 'This dig is not going to be prejudiced by your timetable.'

'Hey, hang on. This meeting's in your interests.'

'In what way?'

'We're discussing putting in the cash to do a facial reconstruction on the skull. Wouldn't you like to see that?'

Yes, thought Patrick, more than anything. 'No,' he said. 'It's old hat, isn't it? They're always doing that on TV.'

'We've got the chance of going a bit further,' retorted Camden, stung. 'That's what I have to go and talk about.'

By mutual, silent consent, Patrick, CD and Dozer went very slowly, making a meal of every aspect of the recording. What was emerging from the soil was an intricate beaker of pale blue-green glass, the conical cup part ornamented by two tiers of curving glass arches. When the top half had been exposed and Camden had taken Jack and his camera away, Patrick called everyone over to see it. Bobby, who had been down at the farm cooking a curry that Dozer had already labelled Indian stew, was walking back up the hill, and Patrick waited until she joined them.

'Quite a day,' he said. 'We'll try to draw some conclusions

tonight, but I just want to bring you all up to date on what we've found. We now know that she was indeed buried on a wooden bed and the latest thing to show up is a wonderful piece of glass, this clawed beaker.' As a joke, he called across, 'Peter, I don't suppose you know anything about clawed beakers, do you?'

It didn't occur to Peter for one moment to take it as a joke. 'A bit,' he said. 'They're Saxon copies of a Roman style of beaker, but if you look at those curved supports running up from the base, the Saxon version is much cruder. The Roman ones often have dolphin shapes where the Saxons just used plain arcs of glass.'

'Thank you,' said Patrick. 'Now, these beakers are very often found in pairs, so with a bit of luck we might even find its twin tomorrow.'

Bobby had crouched down by the edge of the trench and was staring at the beaker.

'That's it for now,' Patrick said. 'Clear up your loose and get yourselves cleaned up. After supper we'll have the fireside chat again.'

An hour later, showered and changed into slightly cleaner jeans, Patrick was sitting outside his tent, brooding on the day.

A voice, Bobby's, broke in. 'Would you like a glass of wine?'

'I would. Thank you.' He took the glass she held out.

'You're not very observant, are you?' she said.

It was the sort of thing Rachel used to say in their early days when she'd had her hair done or bought new clothes. He stared at Bobby. Not her hair—she wore the same concealing woollen hat. Not her clothes. 'What have I missed?' he said cautiously. She was watching him like a hawk. He raised the glass to his lips and she raised her eyebrows. He realised the lip of the glass was very thick and the stem was an intricate and bulky affair. He looked at what he was holding—it was the clawed beaker from the grave.

He stared at it, bewildered. 'What have you done? You haven't taken it out? Don't you realise—'

She was shaking her head. 'It's still there,' she said. 'Just don't raise your hopes when you go looking for the matching one. You're already holding it.'

'This is the other one? How can it be? I mustn't drink *wine* out of it,' Patrick said, holding the beaker as carefully as possible.

'Why not?' she replied. 'That's what I've been doing for years. We've had it in the house ever since I can remember. I suppose it's something Dad found in a rabbit hole. I thought it was maybe Victorian or something until I saw the one in the grave.' She giggled. 'It's even been in the dishwasher.'

'You must have realised it was special, surely?'

Bobby shrugged. 'The house is stacked with Dad's stuff, everything he ever found. Joe spends a lot of time looking at it. You'll have to come and see it all.'

'Definitely. When shall I come?'

'After supper? No, that won't do. After the fireside chat.'

Patrick imagined the two of them walking off together into the dark and the whispering that would start all over again. He could suggest CD came too but he didn't want to. He wanted the chance to look at this stuff all by himself first, whatever it was.

'Fine,' he said, 'after the fireside chat.'

The curry didn't hold anyone's attention for very long.

'Undercooked British root vegetable vindaloo,' pronounced CD when he was sure Bobby couldn't hear. 'Executed with a certain panache or maybe it was potash, I couldn't be certain.'

Round the fire, Aidan spoke first. 'Our lady there—don't you think she was a bit of a sport? That gaming board stuff. She was competitive, I think—someone who'd give the boys a run for their money. I like a woman like that.'

Patrick sat in the dark listening, thinking of the women he'd turned to when life became exciting. Women who egged him on, who played pool, who drove aggressively and evoked a powerful response. He was astonished by how foreign all that felt now. That was not the nature of the woman of Wytchlow, this brave soul whose values were straightforward matters of life, death and loyalty, whose vitality had reached out to touch them all from the grave.

'Aidan's right,' said Maxwell. 'She's like Zelda. A real warrior woman. I bet she was beautiful.'

'Who on earth is Zelda?' said Gaye.

'Don't you know Zelda? The video game?'

'No, I most certainly do not.'

'I didn't say she was like that,' said Aidan, affronted. 'She was a good woman, wasn't she? Not some kind of a cartoon. I just meant she enjoyed a laugh or they wouldn't have put the game in there. I agree with old Maxwell though, I bet she was a beauty.'

'We might find out,' Patrick said cautiously. 'Kenny Camden's talking about doing a facial reconstruction.'

'Does that take a long time?'

'Not if we get her skull out in one piece.'

'Take her head off?' said Gaye aghast. 'That's horrible. I was thinking we'd, well . . . we'd keep her together. Treat her properly. I'm starting to see what that vicar means. While her bones are lying there, she's still a person, isn't she? Are we really going to take them apart?'

'We have to take the bones out of the grave. They need proper examination. They come out one at a time.'

To change the subject, Dozer turned to Bobby. 'Any chance of seeing your bro tonight, love?'

'I don't think so,' she said. 'He was loading up his backpack when I left. That usually means he's going to be off somewhere all night.'

'Where does he go?'

'I haven't a clue. He's always back by morning to start work.'

'Shame that. I was looking forward to another surprise.' Dozer spoke for them all.

The talk seemed to run out of steam after that.

'Might go down the pub,' said Dozer.

'Good plan,' said CD. 'Who's coming?'

Everyone was, except Patrick and Bobby.

'I might come later,' Patrick said. 'I've got a few things to do.'

Bobby took the dirty dishes down the hill in the Land Rover. When the others had all gone to the village, Patrick walked down after her, telling himself his anticipation was all about her father's finds.

As he came round the corner towards the gate, Patrick saw the tail-lights of a car swinging into the road. Bobby was standing in the yard looking furious.

'What's the matter?' he said.

'Roger bloody Little, our so-called Chairman of Governors.'

'Your friend and mine. What did he want?'

She waved the letter she was holding. 'He's given me notice that they're applying for a court injunction to stop us taking the children out of school for May Day. It's just vindictive, that's all.'

'You can fight it, can't you? There must be a hearing of some sort. You can give your side.'

'Oh sure. Just imagine how that will be. Me and a few of the mothers against three pillars of society? Can you imagine any judge taking the slightest notice of us? I haven't got any evidence.' He realised she was on the edge of tears.

'I'll help you. In any way I can.'

She shook her head. 'Come on in. Sorry, that wasn't much of a welcome. Would you like another glass of wine?'

'Out of an ordinary glass?' he said to try to make her laugh.

'I can probably run to plastic if you're happier with it.'

The wide front door led into a big, stone-flagged hallway with a beamed ceiling. The hall was lit only by a dim bulb and she led him through to a big kitchen with an old roughly painted Aga and a huge table covered in cracked Formica. He followed her into another room almost filled by a rug-covered sofa and two old brown armchairs.

'Have a look. I'll get the wine.'

The walls were completely lined with shelving on which sat a hotchpotch of dusty objects. Patrick stood in front of them, staring. He picked up a tiny pottery oil lamp with a hand grip at one side, clearly Roman. Next to the lamp was half a medieval floor-tile, inlaid with a fleur-de-lis pattern.

'It's not great wine, I'm afraid,' said Bobby, coming back in with two glasses.

'I'm sure it's fine,' Patrick said, taking a sip and discovering she was right. He was staring at two small bronze pyramids, an inch or so across, decorated with some sort of filigree work. He picked one of them up. 'Look at these,' he said. 'They're Saxon. Part of a scabbard, I think. Where did they come from?'

'I haven't a clue.' She was preoccupied. 'Have you any idea what happens if you break an injunction?'

'We could ask Peter,' he said, and won a smile out of her. 'I think it's pretty serious stuff if you do because it's contempt of court. Don't go *that* far, will you? It's not worth it.'

'You don't know that. I keep wondering what *she* would have done.'

'Our woman in the grave?'

'Yes. I'm pretty sure she wouldn't have let them stop her.'

'I'm sure she wouldn't, but you're not going to take your sword to the vicar, are you?'

'Just give me the chance! Anyway, that's not why you're here. What do you think of our collection?'

'Extraordinary. You should get a professional to have a look at it.'

'I have. You're here. Joe wouldn't want lots of strangers going over this stuff, but I know he approves of you.'

'What makes you think he approves of me?'

'I just know it.' She looked at him, so full of crackling life that he felt a spark would jump across if he stretched out a hand. 'My mum used to say Joe had appointed himself guardian of Dad's treasures. I once broke a little bowl and he got so upset.'

'Was it something special?'

'I don't know. He mended it. It's here somewhere.'

She searched the shelves. Standing with her back to Patrick, her figure and her way of holding herself seemed to him so like Rachel that he longed to get up and put his arms round her and bury his face in her neck.

She turned round and raised her eyebrows at whatever it was she saw in his face. 'Is something wrong?' she said.

He took a step and his arms came out to her and he saw her eyes widen. He stopped then and looked down at the bowl and took that instead. 'Late medieval,' he said in a voice he didn't recognise.

'Um . . . is it? You can see where Joe mended it. It's the only time he's ever been cross with me. He was Dad's boy.'

'What happened to your mum?'

'She died three years ago. That's when I had to come back and help Joe run the farm. He couldn't do it on his own.'

'Come back? Where from?'

'A long way away and another world completely.'

'What were you doing?'

She shut off abruptly. 'It's not the right time for life stories.'

'I didn't mean to—'

'You don't want to talk about yours. I don't want to talk about mine. Isn't that fair?'

'I suppose so.' All at once, he could feel how it hurt to be shut out. 'I know I've probably been fairly unreasonable to you.'

'I have to admit it is hard when you suddenly treat me like your worst enemy. Can you tell me why you do that?'

'Oh dear,' he said. 'There's something I find very difficult to tell you, something that would explain it.'

He looked at the shelves, searching for the right words to start. His gaze fell on a photo of a man in some kind of tunic, smiling at the camera. 'Who's this?' he said, picking it up.

She took it out of his grasp. 'You tell me this difficult thing of yours, in full, with nothing left out, and if I think you've told me enough I'll decide whether to answer that question.'

'All right,' he said, but he still didn't know if he could do it. 'The thing is . . .'

She stood waiting.

'The reason I have behaved rather, well . . . oddly towards you is that I find just looking at you really disturbing. You look so like Rachel that I keep getting you muddled up.'

'I look like your wife?'

'*Exactly* like her. Well, exactly like she would have looked by now if I had treated her better. If I hadn't drained everything that mattered out of her.'

She was shaking her head. 'So what does that mean? I'm a painful reminder? Are you saying you can't bear to look at me, or what?'

'No, not that. You just take me straight back to the last time life was good, to the time when I was in love with Rachel. Every time I look at you, for a moment it's like life's given me another chance and then I realise it hasn't.'

She turned her face away. 'That's a heavy responsibility to put on me, Patrick. I'm not her and I'm nothing to do with your guilt.' She frowned. 'Actually, what you've just said pisses me off a bit. I've been quite glad that I seemed to be someone you felt you could talk to. I wanted to see if I could help. I thought we had some sort of point of contact. Now it seems we don't. I've looked at you when you've been looking at me and there's been something between us. Now you're saying it's all just an accident caused by the shape of my nose or something. That's not very flattering.'

He almost said there was much more to it than that, but reason once again overcame his emotion.

'I'm sorry if I've managed to upset you again.'

'Part of your problem,' she said, 'might just be that you think you're the only person in the world who has been through it. Well, I don't feel like telling you about this—' she waved the photo at him—'because I don't suppose it can possibly match up to what's happened to you, not for a moment.'

'I'd like to hear about him,' Patrick said quietly.

'Well, I'll just give you the headlines. He's . . .' Her voice caught. 'He was somebody I was in love with. He got sick. I couldn't save him. He died. Right? Is that enough for now? One death for me, two deaths for you. You lead two to one.'

'Bobby, I am so—'

'No, no, no. Let's not get into who's sorrier than who. Let's just call it quits and get some sleep. You know the way out.'

He was halfway across the yard with his heart in his boots when he heard an upper window open.

'Patrick,' she called.

He turned and she was silhouetted in a dormer window.

'Yes?'

Her voice was softer and a little hesitant. 'I just wanted to say you should keep an ear open tonight. There's been a bit too much talk round the village, a few hotheads talking about all the stuff you're supposed to have found. I'd be happier if I knew you were watching out.'

She wants the night to end on a different note, he thought. He felt grateful. 'OK, I'll listen out. Sleep well.'

Of course, after that, it was hard to sleep. The others disturbed him coming back from the pub and he lay on his back wishing he'd found words that might have gone down better. It was hard when he knew he mustn't let her think he was attracted to her. That wouldn't be fair. It wasn't her he was attracted to, it was just a ghost. Such thoughts became intolerable, and he decided to get out of the tent and walk round the hilltop.

The remains of the moon shone through fringes of cloud. In that tricky light, the square silhouette of the grave cover seemed to be moving against the sky. He walked towards it and saw it *was* moving.

As fast and as quietly as he could he approached the trench. Now he could see the cover stood to one side of it and close by there were two figures rushing towards each other. He heard the sound of a fist landing on flesh, a cry and then another blow.

'Stop,' he shouted, then both of the figures were running away and he was racing after them. He caught the nearer one easily, tripped the man with his leg and fell on top of him.

'Get off me,' said a woman's voice.

'Bobby? Oh shit. Sorry. Did he hurt you?'

'Not nearly as much as you did.'

Torchlights were coming from the tents now.

'Who's that?' shouted Dozer.

'Me, Patrick,' he shouted back. 'There was a guy trying to nick stuff. He's run off towards the village.'

'Right, I'll 'ead 'im off at the pass,' shouted Dozer. 'Come on, CD, you ride shotgun.' He lumbered towards his car with CD in pursuit.

'I heard two blows.'

'You did,' she said, sounding pleased with herself. 'The first one was me punching him in the eye. It wouldn't surprise me if Roger Little doesn't keep his face well out of sight for a few days.'

'It was Little? Really? Why would he be up here?'

'Because he's a greedy man who wants a bit of everything and it's probably been driving him mad wondering what we might be finding up here.'

'But why were you up here? You asked *me* to listen out.'

'I don't think you really believed me, did you?'

'I suppose you're right. You usually are about most things,' said

Patrick. 'Well, you can go home and get some proper sleep now. I'll move my tent up here in the morning.'

'And the rest of tonight?'

He looked at the grave cover. 'If we put this back over it, there's enough room for me to sleep inside. I'll get my sleeping-bag.'

NINE

Patrick woke to find the ground drumming against his ear. The earth was telegraphing solid footfalls coming at him in the darkness. He was disorientated, aware immediately that he was in an unfamiliar place, then he recognised that he and the German Queen had been sleeping side by side. He sat up, holding his breath. The footsteps were coming from the far side of the hill.

A pale shadow was now looming up against the tent fabric and he felt he was only moments away from violence or horror.

The footsteps stopped, the shadow collapsed to half its height as if kneeling, and a man's voice began to sing quietly outside.

'There came the time of the old King's death
And he blessed her with his final breath.
He gave his sword to be handed down
For the boy who would one day wear his crown.

They buried him at the battle stone,
And the news went out that he had gone.
Far to the east, the traitors heard
Of the end of the King with the chicken sword.

The Queen again grew big with child
As it turned to winter, calm and mild.
She woke one night from a warning dream
And heard the watchman's dying scream.

Her husband left their bed so warm
And summoned men to brave the storm.
She dressed herself in a warrior's cloak
And the chicken sword from the wall she took.

Two hours they fought on that bloody hill
And the chicken sword's blade drank its fill.
They stood their ground in the Bury Field,
Outnumbered, they refused to yield.

Three to two they stood at last
On the burying place from a distant past.
There she fought like a bear for her children's life
And for one unborn in the midst of strife.

The traitors struck a mortal blow
That felled her lord on the witch's low.
She whirled the blade like an iron fan
And two more fell to join her man.

Right to the end on the blood-soaked grass,
She would not let those traitors pass.
Just one more faced her, towering tall,
The villains' leader, worst of all.

He cut her down with a coward's blow
Struck from behind and it laid her low.
They found her there, still holding tight
To the chicken sword in its final fight.'

Joe, back from his wanderings and unaware that he was overheard, was paying a visit to the German Queen. When the singing ended, Patrick wondered whether Joe would open the flap and, if he did, whether he would be embarrassed to find he had an audience.

Then Joe spoke.

'I've come to say I'm sorry, Queen,' he said, and Patrick, astonished, strained to listen, knowing it was far too late to reveal his presence. When he thought no one alive could hear him, Joe, it seemed, could find words.

'The thing is, I don't know if I need to or not. I brought them here, it's true, and they've disturbed you, but they know that you're special because I've made sure they know your story. Anyway, I can't help thinking that what was really you has gone into this whole hilltop now. They've disturbed your bones but bones weren't what you laughed with and loved with and fought with. They were just . . . the easel on which your picture was drawn. Oh yes, my dad told me what his dad told him—that you were really something. He said that when you died it must have been like a punch in the guts for all those who loved you, a punch that takes the wind out of you when you know that you shouldn't have taken all those moments for granted and that now there is just the bitter ache of the lonely future. That's why they put you up here, where they could look up at your mound every day from where they lived. Anyway, my lady, I think those other parts that were really you have gone into the ground here and they've helped make a million blades of grass and a great sprawl of flowers every year and those have seeded and spread and carried you across all the hills so I hope you don't mind what's happened too much.'

Then he walked off. When Patrick had heard the last of his footsteps, he unzipped the tent flap and looked out. On the grass in front of him was a bunch of spring flowers in a jar. He went back inside, holding them, moved by what he'd heard and, looking down at the skeletons in the grave, put the flowers at the head of the trench.

He stared at her and tried to imagine her and of course he failed. Instead, Joe's words came back to him: "a punch that takes the wind out of you"; "the bitter ache of the lonely future".

Loss, when it came to Patrick in Perugia, had a shape to it, a long balloon inflating upwards from his stomach through his chest cavity, driving a prickling blizzard of tears ahead of it. It had a sound too, a shout that burst out of him, as loud as he could make it, but never loud enough to drain the pain.

'I wasn't any good as a father,' he said out loud to the woman in the grave. 'I meant to be a good father. I was going to be better. I was ready to change. I was going back to say "I'm sorry" to them both. Poor Rachel. I broke her. There was no excuse for that.'

He stood there in silence for a while, staring at the skeleton.

Next to her lay the sword, her father's great sword. Seeing the first light of dawn through the tent covering and knowing there would be no more sleep that night, he went to get his trowel. In the next two hours he excavated the last part of the sword, the hand-guard.

There were swirling patterns of silver inlaid along the edges of a broad iron guard, a thick bar across the top of the blade.

The tang of the blade passed through the hole in the guard and, at the other end of the hand-grip, was clenched tightly into the pommel, a smaller bar with faint decoration just visible. The scabbard fittings he'd seen at Bobby's house could have gone with this sword.

'CD's got to see this before I do any more,' said Patrick out loud.

'CD's snoring in his tent,' said Bobby behind him.

Patrick spun round. 'Hello. How embarrassing, to be caught talking to our friend here.'

'It would have been rude not to,' said Bobby.

'Yes.' Should he tell her of the astonishing visit from her brother? He looked at her and saw the purple swelling on her cheek.

'Let me have a look at that,' he said. He took a step towards her, reached out his hand and felt it gently. 'Does it hurt?'

'Only when you press it,' she said, and he pulled his hand away sharply. 'Joke,' she added. 'Anyway, I came to say it was my turn to apologise. It was just a bad day yesterday, that's all.'

'There's no need. It was very brave of you to go for our intruder.'

'Well, I'd better go and get the food on.'

'Bobby. Wait a minute.' He'd reached a decision. 'Joe was here this morning. He scared the hell out of me until I realised it was him. The thing is, he didn't know I was inside here and I heard him. He spoke. He was kneeling outside and talking to her completely normally. He was apologising for the fact that we're disturbing her.'

'Did he speak for long?' she said incredulously.

'Well, yes. He said some very beautiful things. He said her bones were just an easel on which her body had been painted and that the grass and flowers were her real remains. You're crying.'

'I can't help it. I know he does do that. I've sometimes heard him when he thinks I'm asleep. I only *wish* he could talk to me.' She blinked the tears away. 'No, I'm glad. I always knew there was a lot going on in his mind. Did he find out you were here?'

'No. I think he'd be horrified if he knew I'd heard. Bobby, that reminds me. The night they got me singing, why were you crying?'

'Oh, it's complicated.'

'Try me.'

'Well, first my heart was in my mouth because I could see you had started to sing something that was painful for you. Then you stopped and played that other stuff and I suddenly saw the real Patrick. You just lost yourself in the music and it was beautiful.'

'And that made you cry?'

'Almost. Not quite. No, it was something you sang. It just happened to be a very painful song for me.'

'Do you want to tell me?'

'No, some other time. I've got breakfast to do. Play for us again before this is all over, won't you?'

'Only if you tell me what songs I mustn't sing.'

'No, we can't lead our lives that way. We just have to learn to hear them differently.'

A CONVOY OF CARS brought Hescroft, Camden, Jack and an unfamiliar iron-haired woman just as the diggers were ready to start work.

'This is Celia Longworth,' said Hescroft. 'She's our bone person.'

Patrick brought them up-to-date about the sword. 'It's a very fine weapon, according to CD. He says there's one almost identical to it in the Ashmolean and two in the British Museum.'

They collected the American and went up the hill to look at it, and when she saw it Celia Longworth gave a cry of excitement.

'Yes!' she said. 'My goodness me, you're quite right. It is very, very like the earlier of the Abingdon swords. The blade's in even better condition. What superb metal they must have used.'

Hescroft had other things on his mind. 'Patrick,' he said, 'Kenny here has some good news. He's picked up serious coproduction money from US Cable and Northern TV. We've got the green light to go from development into production and, what's more, we've got a budget that buys a few tricks.'

'What it means, Pat,' said Kenny Camden, 'is that we can do something pretty serious about your bones. You tell him, Celia.'

She looked at him with a knowing expression that said she was a professional and that she shared his clear distaste at the bullshit. 'Well, Patrick, of course you'll be familiar with facial reconstruction, building up muscle layers over the skull and working out the main dimensions through computer scanning programs.'

'Yes, I've seen them.'

'We've just gone one stage further in my unit. We've started analysing muscle attachment markings and joint articulation in the skeleton itself and we're finding we can get very realistic animation.'

CD whistled. 'You can make her walk around realistically?'

'What does that mean you have to do to our skeleton?' asked Patrick nervously.

'We just put all the bones through a three-D scanner. May I see the skeleton? I'll need to assess whether it's practical.'

They moved the tent for her. It felt oddly disturbing to see someone who wasn't directly involved going down into the trench.

'Bone preservation's very good,' Celia Longworth said after a long inspection. 'Everything's here except some toe bones on one foot. The foetus is amazingly intact apart from the skull. I'd say this is the ideal candidate. When can we lift it?'

'This morning, I suppose,' Patrick said. He hated the idea of putting her bit by bit into a box. 'Everything's exposed now except the lower part of the skull. That shouldn't take long. One thing, though,' he added. 'We all feel we would like to bury her and the child properly afterwards, up here, where she belongs.'

'Yes, that's right,' said CD, who hadn't heard a word of this before. 'We all feel very strongly that would be the right thing to do.'

'Sounds pretty good to me,' said Kenny Camden. 'A touching ending, I'd say.'

Later that morning, Patrick lifted the bones, carefully and with a heavy heart, one by one into the padded boxes they had labelled and prepared. Lifting the baby's crushed skull, a piece at a time with tweezers, was the worst of it and no one who was watching made a sound while he did it. When he finally wriggled his fingers delicately underneath the mother's skull to lift it, he felt the gap in the bone that explained why they had laid her with her head on one side: so that the terrible injury that had killed her would be hidden.

'SHE DIED FROM A VIOLENT downward blow to the left side of her head,' said Patrick that night round the campfire.

Joe was sitting in earshot but a little outside the circle.

'Would it have been . . . quick?' asked Gaye.

'I would have thought so,' said Patrick, because he'd asked himself the same question as he'd held the skull.

'What's Celia Longworth done with the skeletons?' Gaye asked. 'It really doesn't feel at all right, not having them here.'

There was a general murmur of agreement.

'I asked her from all of us if she would take special care,' Patrick said. 'She's laid them out, side by side on the examination table.'

'So what happens now?' said Dozer. 'Clean up and fill in?'

'No, it's a bit more than that. Camden wants to keep us all here for two or three days more while the labs do their work. So he can have us responding to it all on camera, I suppose. There's the message sword and the real sword to be cleaned and all the other small finds. Then there's this reconstruction and DNA testing they're going to do on the skeleton.'

There was something else Patrick couldn't bring himself to tell them about, revealed to him that afternoon.

'I'VE GOT A BIT of a dilemma you can help me out with, Pat,' Camden had said in a quiet corner of the Oxford lab. 'Let's get a cuppa and talk it through.'

Patrick smelt another attempt at a set-up.

They got plastic cups of not-quite tea from a machine in the hallway and Patrick sat down by the window. Outside, the traffic was stationary on the Cowley Road. His flat was less than a mile away and the thought that he would soon be spending his nights in it alone filled him with despair. He knew all at once that he'd become very fond of his bunch of diggers.

Camden perched on the windowsill. 'You know the way it is with networks,' he said as if Patrick was an old colleague. We've got the Yanks and the Aussies in it now and they both want human interest, you understand?'

'All too well,' said Patrick wearily. 'You still want to do the rock star angle, right?'

'No, no,' said Camden with an expression that said he was astonished that Patrick could ever have thought such a thing. 'It would have been great, sure, but I've had to respect your wishes. No, I've been looking around for a different human interest line and I think I've found something that's nearly as good. Well, three things really.'

'Oh? What are they?'

'OK. First there's the vicar and all this business of giving the bodies a Christian burial. You wouldn't have any objections to making that part of the film, would you? We'd have to film a bit of a ding-dong between the two of you.'

To Patrick it seemed a relatively small price to pay for his continued anonymity.

'No, I don't think I'd mind that.'

'So far so good. Then that leads on to this business about the vicar and the headmaster and the chick who's cooking for you.'

'The May Day parade? How could that fit in?'

'Oh, you know, village traditions. We'll find a way. While you're waking up the past on top of the hill, the headmaster's trying to put it to bed down in the village, something like that.'

'That would be up to Bobby. I don't know she'd want to do it.'

'Well, it's not her decision; it's a story; it's out there; it's public property. They're in court the day after tomorrow, aren't they? But leave that for now. It's her brother I really want.'

Her brother? Oh no. 'Why's that?'

'Now that's a *really* powerful story line. Anonymous archaeologist, down on his luck, listens to a song sung in a pub by the local weirdo and lo and behold, it all turns out to be true. You dig up the woman, you dig up the sword. Bingo, I've got a story the Yanks will love. The German Queen comes out of the grave. It's brilliant. It'll be great TV. Thing is, I need you to persuade the bloke to sing it again. We could use it as a soundtrack.'

Bobby will flip her lid, Patrick thought. She'll think I put them up to this to get myself out of the trap the TV man had sprung. 'There's something else you could do instead,' he suggested in desperation. 'This local builder, Little—the guy who wrecked the first site—why not bring him into it? Bobby caught someone trying to nick stuff from the trench last night. She's sure it was Little.'

'Oh please. You must know a bit about the laws of libel. You got any proof at all that it was him who did the damage? A local issue, that's not going to play too well in Peoria.'

'Where?'

'Just an expression. Cleveland, Boston, Wollongong, wherever. What do they care about a builder and a few square yards of flooring? A mute farmer with a direct line to history, now that's something else.'

That was when Celia Longworth came looking for them.

'You wanted my first impressions,' she said. 'She was in the prime of life. Maybe twenty-five. Quite tall, about five foot nine, and in good health. No sign of infections, breaks or disease on the bones.'

'And the wound?' asked Patrick.

'It looks like a single blow but I'll have a better idea when we've done a full examination. I'll let you know.'

After that, Patrick went to his flat to get another pair of jeans. There was only one letter on the mat, a royalty cheque, revealing the unwelcome news that two of Nam Erewhon's albums had taken on a new lease of life in the Far East. He left it on the kitchen table. He'd decide later what charity to send it to.

'IF ANYBODY'S DYING TO LEAVE, they can,' said Patrick that evening around the campfire, 'but Hescroft's agreed that we should widen the trench to check for anything we've missed.'

'And what might be the point of this DNA testing stuff?' said Aidan.

'It doesn't really help the archaeology,' said Patrick, 'but apparently it's the sort of stuff that makes good TV. The idea is you might find descendants.'

'So are they going to test us?' said Dozer.

'Not much point testing you,' said CD. 'You've clearly got no human ancestry whatsoever.'

'So there could be people still living in Wytchlow who are the great-great-great-times-a-hundred-grandsons of our Queen?' said Maxwell.

Peter cleared his throat and a reverent hush fell. 'It does have to be mitochrondial DNA,' he said. 'That means it comes down the mother's line. So there could be a man living in the village related to our Queen, but the ancestry would have to be through his mother and his mother's mother and so on.'

Maxwell turned to Peter. 'And it survives that long?'

'Oh, they've got DNA from Neanderthal man dating back over fifty thousand years.'

'Cool,' said Maxwell, 'but our Queen's baby died with her, surely? So how could she have any female descendants?'

'She might have had other kids before,' said Aidan.

'She *did* have others,' Gaye said indignantly. 'We know that, don't we? From Joe's song. You know, the one we all did by the grave.'

They turned to look at Joe, sitting outside the circle, and he, in that same half-chanting, half-singing style, repeated the opening lines: 'The boda came to Abbandun at evening bell, Brought by the child with sunset head.'

'It doesn't say it was her child,' said Aidan.

Joe nodded downwards, just once, and nobody felt like arguing.

'And what do you suppose those words mean, that sunset head thing?' said Aidan, to show willing.

'I'd like to think it means the child had hair like a sunset,' said Gaye. 'Wild hair, sticking out like rays of light, probably golden. That sounds more like a girl than a boy, so you see Peter's mito-whatever it was could easily have come down from her, couldn't it?'

'That's reading quite a lot into a single word,' said Peter.

'Well, I think I'm right,' said Gaye defiantly.

'That's my girl,' said Dozer. 'You tell 'em.'

'I'm not your girl and I never will be.'

'I'm proud of old Gaye here,' said Dozer. 'Do you know why?'

'Stop it,' she said. 'You promised you wouldn't tell anybody.'

'Dropped her hairbrush down the carzey this morning. Reached in and got it out. I found her giving it a wash.'

There was a round of applause and Gaye gave a shrug and a little smile. 'It's the only one I had,' she said.

'Sorts out the women from the girls, this kind of thing,' said Dozer. 'Here, speaking of women, where's Bobby? A campfire ain't a campfire without our Bobby.'

'She's down at the house. She said she'd be up soon,' said Gaye. 'I asked her to pick up some wine. It's on me tonight.'

There was a cheer which disturbed Edgar down in CD's tent. He cawed indignantly.

'You got your keys back from that tree yet?' Dozer asked CD.

'I'm borrowing a ladder tomorrow.'

'Look for my ring while you're up there,' said Gaye. 'He flew off with it this morning.'

'Raven burgers,' said CD. 'Imagine how tasty they would be.'

Bobby's old Land Rover groaned out of the twilight and she came over to Patrick. 'Special request,' she said. 'If I find you a guitar, will you play for us again?'

He found to his astonishment that something had changed. He could think of playing without any of the old associations being stirred in his mind. 'Only if it's not Maxwell's,' he said. 'My fingers are still recovering.'

'Wait a moment,' she said.

She walked back to the Land Rover and produced a padded guitar case. The instrument that came out of it shone deep golden brown and she passed it to Patrick, holding it flat out with both hands like an offering. It was a classical jazz guitar, oozing hand-made quality, and when he rippled his thumb across the strings, the sound they produced was exceptional.

'This is something else,' he said. Then he noticed the way Bobby was looking at him, and he knew that this was an emotional moment for her, a bridge of some sort she had decided to cross.

'Who made it?' he asked, trying to see if there was a label inside.

'Don't ask questions. Just go on. Play.'

So Patrick got them all singing, his own voice leading them like the Pied Piper, with Joe joining in with a deep bass. It was an evening spun from magic. When, at last, the wine was gone and the fire was dying down, Patrick walked back to the Land Rover with Bobby, and put the guitar back carefully inside.

'Thank you,' he said as she got in. 'It's got a story to it, hasn't it?'

She nodded.

'Would you tell me?'

'Why do you want to know?'

'Because I think you might want me to. Isn't that why you let me play it?'

'Perhaps,' she said. 'I don't know what I can say about it.'

'It's up to you.'

'I'm not sure I shut up the chicken house,' she said, looking away from him, down to the farm. 'I've got to go back and check.'

He thought that was the end of it but she turned back. 'Give me ten minutes. I'll meet you. Where the track takes you down to the yard, follow it on and there's a slope up into an old orchard above the vegetable garden. There's a sort of shelter with a bench in it.'

'HE CAME FROM QUEBEC, like the guitar,' she said without a word of preamble, when he found her sitting on the bench in the dark and sat down close to her. 'He was called Gilles and he worked with me and he died.' She was looking straight in front of her. A light in a window of the farmhouse showed him her profile.

'It was his guitar?'

'Yes, it was his guitar.'

'Why did you let me play it tonight?'

'Because you can play it nearly as well as he could but, more importantly, because this is all about attitudes to life.' She hesitated, then went on more forcefully. 'When something goes really wrong you have the choice, don't you? Leaving out suicide, you can either curl up inside your shell or you can go out and get on with it. What do you see when you look at me? I mean when you look at me—Bobby—not at some awful old memory.'

'I see someone who gets on with it, someone who all my diggers would happily go to jail for if the vicar got in her way.'

'When I look at you it seems to me that you're somewhere between the two, the curling up and the getting on with it. With a bit of a heave from your friends, you're just starting to come out of your shell, and I think it's time you started thinking about other people more.'

He was shocked. 'What do you mean?'

'I mean that nobody lives on this earth in a vacuum. You can be as miserable as you like by yourself but when you do it in company you take other people down with you. I don't think anyone has the right to be such a misery as you are. You've had the whole lot of them, CD, Dozer, everybody, tiptoeing round you for most of this dig, not sure whether you're going to fly off the handle or burst into tears on them.'

'God Almighty. I'm not that bad, am I?'

'And some. Well, you *were*, anyway. I have to admit there are slight signs of improvement.'

'Look, if I am that bad, I'm sorry, but I'm not sure I can always help it. You know why. I told you.'

'Your wife and son died. You said something you shouldn't have and *she* drove off the road. She did that, not you. It was a tragedy, but it's time to get it in proportion. You can't trail it around behind you for the rest of your life.'

'How did Gilles die?'

'We were working together. In the southern Sudan. There was a French-Canadian medical charity. Gilles was one of the doctors.'

'What were you doing, nursing?'

'Oh, sod off, Patrick.'

'What have I said now?'

'I was a doctor too.'

'I see.'

'That's why some of them round here think I'm a bit full of myself for a farmer's daughter. Anyway, we were cut off for a long time in a village, Gilles and me. There was a civil war going on all around us. We had a radio but a soldier put a pickaxe through it and we were running out of everything, and then Gilles got sick.'

She fell silent and Patrick prompted her gently. 'And you couldn't help him?'

'If I had a hospital lab, I could have done. If I could have found out what it was. All I had to go on was what I could see and I just couldn't tell for sure. He'd been on a trip out with one of the village men. When he came back he was confused and drowsy. The guy he was with thought maybe he'd fallen over. He had this bruise and swelling. I thought it was a subdural haematoma. Bleeding under the skull. But his pupils were different sizes and he had a fever. He shouldn't have had a fever. So maybe it was cerebral malaria, one of the few things I still had drugs for.'

'Did they work? The drugs?'

'No.' She sounded so sad, frightened. 'He just went on getting worse. I was going to fly him out on a supply plane. It didn't come on the day it was meant to. I waited all the next day. I was beside myself. All I could do was try to get liquids into him. In the early evening one of the village boys came running in and told me they could hear the plane. I went outside and we could see it, maybe half a mile off over some scrubland. Then I saw sparks flying up towards it like a firework and it veered away. Two or three seconds later I heard a burst of machine-gun fire from the scrub.'

'The plane was shot down?'

'No, it was just damaged, but it turned away.' She was speaking slowly. 'So then I knew I hadn't got any alternative. I thought it must be the haematoma after all, and there's only one thing to do with a haematoma. You have to drill a hole in the skull, to relieve the pressure of the bleeding. I drilled a hole in my lovely man's skull.' She sighed. 'There was no haematoma. Then before the plane finally came back five days later, he got meningitis because of what I did and . . . and he died.'

'Oh, Bobby.' His overpowering instinct was to put his arm round her, but she was far away with her dead lover and he could not. 'There wasn't anything else you could do, though, was there?'

'Do you think that helps?' she said grimly. 'Do you think when you love someone with all your heart and you're making plans to go back to Quebec together it helps to know that?'

'No. I'm so sorry.'

Her tone changed, became brisker. 'I didn't tell you so that you'd be sorry. The point of my little story is that life goes on. I got out a week later. I was back in Khartoum, then there was a call from Jean Anderson down in the village telling me Mum was in hospital. So I came back and I was just in time to see her and then I realised I had to stay for Joe, so now that's what we do. We farm, day in, day out. When I heard about the dig, I thought: great, I'll have some fun. I didn't realise the dig director was going to come fitted with his own personal thundercloud. All the people who came on this dig, they all deserve something better, not just me.'

'Oh shit.' The weight of it hit him. 'I'd been living in my head for too long. This is the first time I've been out in public for ages. I'm doing better than I was, surely?'

'Most of the time. What was bugging you tonight when I arrived? I could see it in your face.'

'I had a difficult time with Camden. He wants me in his programme. Me, as Paddy Kane, punk rocker. Just to boost the ratings.'

'And you've told him to take a running jump.'

'It's not that simple. He says he needs a human-interest angle and if it's not me, he's threatening to use Joe.'

She sat up straight. 'Joe? How could he use Joe?'

'He's heard about the song and how we found the grave.'

'You told Camden that?'

'No, of course not. I didn't tell him. He says someone in the village told him.'

'If you've put him onto Joe to get him off your back I'll never forgive you, Patrick. Don't you dare off-load this onto Joe, OK? I hold you responsible. Good night.'

She got up and walked quickly to the house in the bitter darkness.

TEN

Soon after first light, CD was forty feet up an oak tree, roping himself carefully to the trunk, when he looked through a gap in the branches and saw Patrick in the far distance walking purposefully down towards the farm. The American had risen at the crack of dawn to get his tree-climbing out of the way before anyone else was up and about to laugh at him. He wondered briefly what Patrick was up to, but the tree and the problem of the final six feet to where Edgar had dropped his keys drove other thoughts away. He stretched out for the next handhold, hung precariously by his hands for a moment, and swung a foot onto a safe branch. Three feet left. Before he had fallen out of the tree the last time, he had made a note of the crook of a branch where Edgar had taken his finds. Now he could see that in that crook was an old bird's nest.

He climbed up a little further and lunged upwards with his fingers outstretched. The nest tumbled out of the crook of the branch and he watched it fall, shining objects spilling from it, into the thick leaf mould far below.

When he finally got down to ground level again, he saw his ignition keys lying on the ground and Patrick's pen near them. A bit of searching turned up Gaye's missing ring and he was about to go, pleased with his success, when he just caught the glint of something metallic, almost completely buried in the vegetation.

PATRICK THOUGHT ABOUT what Bobby had said for an hour or two before going to sleep, and when he woke up soon after dawn he went straight to the farm and sat quietly in the yard until he saw a light come on downstairs. Then he knocked on the door.

'Coffee's on the table,' called Bobby from inside.

He walked into the kitchen and she was standing at the Aga, with her back to him.

'Bobby?' he said, and she spun round, staring at him.

'I thought you were Joe. What are you doing here?' She turned back to stir a saucepan.

'I'm here to sort out a couple of things. First, you're right about me wallowing in it. You've made me look at myself. I needed it. Second, I want to say you don't need to worry about Joe. I've decided to tell Camden that so long as he stays completely away from Joe, I'll do it the way he wants. He can have his punk rocker. I've just realised there's no reason it should matter any more.'

'Thank you,' she said. 'Now go. I'm doing Joe's porridge. I'll be up at the camp in fifteen minutes.'

WHEN KENNY CAMDEN'S Toyota appeared after breakfast, Jack was at the wheel and there was no sign of Camden.

'Morning,' Patrick said. 'Where's your boss?'

'Please,' said Jack, grimacing. 'I'm a hungry freelance trying to keep my standards up. I prefer to think of him as my pay cheque. Look, I'm out of line here, but watch him. He's not a nice man.'

'Thanks. I'd sort of guessed. Where is he?'

'Down on the village green. They're setting up the DNA testing.'

Patrick walked off, leaving CD to deal with the trench.

There was a white tent on the green and Camden was standing outside it, talking to the villagers.

'We'll be ready to start at about one o'clock,' Patrick heard him saying. 'Get all your friends to come too. We'll stay open until about seven.' He turned round. 'Morning, Pat. What can I do for you?'

Patrick took him aside. 'I've changed my mind,' he said. 'You can bring me into your programme any way you like.'

'Ha,' said Camden, 'There's still a performer in there, eh? Well, thanks for that, Pat, but no need really. Truth is, I've gone off the idea. Let's face it. Four years is a long time. People have short memories. Sure, I was keen on it to start with but then I thought a bit and, well, it's old hat really, isn't it? I think this farmer guy is a really good story.'

'Joe won't do it.'

'It's not for him to choose. We've already got shots of him.'

'What shots?' said Patrick with a sinking heart.

'You know the way he hangs around the fringes of the dig. I got Jack to watch out for that. It's great. I've managed to put together a few bits and pieces of the song from people who were there, too.'

'I think you're making a mistake.'

'Maybe,' said Camden cheerfully. 'See you back on the hill.'

Patrick couldn't bring himself to tell Bobby what had happened. He spent the rest of the day avoiding her, sitting in his car, writing up the paperwork while the diggers found nothing but two possible Bronze Age potsherds in the barrow ring-ditch.

As suppertime approached, it dawned on him that there was no sign of anything happening in the food tent. He went over and found the diggers inspecting three heaped trays of sandwiches.

'Bobby said she hoped we wouldn't mind,' CD explained. 'She's got some meeting about her protest thing. I said it would be OK.'

'You coming down to the pub?' said Dozer, turning to Patrick. 'Joe's doing another special apparently. Anyway, we're all going to get our DNA done just for a lark. CD's having his changed for something better, like a cockroach.'

'Hey, respect where respect is due, man. Remember, you're looking at a highly successful primate with amazing tree-climbing abilities.'

'You've got your keys back from wherever Edgar took them?' Patrick asked.

'Yup, plus your pen.' He reached into his pocket, 'Gaye's ring and one more thing I am very embarrassed to show you.'

'What?'

CD took out something that glittered dull silver.

'An Anglo-Saxon silver coin, namely one sceatta, almost certainly late seventh century.'

'Which would probably have been extremely useful dating evidence,' said Patrick, 'if we had the remotest idea where on the site it had come from, instead of finding it in a bloody jackdaw's hideaway.'

'He's confined to my tent until we're off the site,' said CD.

THERE WAS A LONG LINE of late arrivals at the DNA tent but the tests were quick. Each person was handed a tiny brush on a stick. It was a simple process. All they had to do was scrub the inside of their cheek, then the brush was put in a sterile bag and labelled.

The pub was packed and the first thing Patrick saw was a large group of women clustered around Bobby. She saw him come in and beckoned to him. He couldn't get right up to her, but she craned her head towards him and said, 'What's going on? They're saying you asked Joe to sing tonight.'

'No, I didn't. I haven't seen him.'

'I heard you sent him a note.' She was frowning.

One of the others turned to her and said, 'Bobby, we all think it should be you who speaks in court,' and she shrugged at Patrick and went back into the conversation.

Joe came into the bar, dressed in his hat and his red waistcoat, and a little cheer ran through the crowd. He sang a song about May Day that was savagely witty at the expense of the head teacher and the vicar. There was a service hatch to the kitchen set in the wall opposite Joe's microphone and Patrick noticed one of the flaps was half open. As the song came to an end, the tip of a camera lens came into view. He knew then that Jack was filming and that the note to Joe must have come from Camden in Patrick's name.

Joe started the introduction to another song and Patrick realised it was the song of the German Queen. He did not want the camera to have it. He started to get to his feet but Joe stopped playing abruptly and marched across to the hatch himself. He reached in, trying to grab the camera. Everybody in the bar started talking at once and there were muffled noises from the other side of the hatch. Joe slammed the hatch shut, turned round and strode out of the pub door.

Patrick saw Bobby rise; the look she gave him was one of hatred. He ducked out of the door into darkness. He would pursue Joe.

But just outside the porch a hand shot out and grabbed Patrick's wrist, and Joe, who had been standing waiting for him, set off round the corner to the car park, towing him along.

'I didn't send that note,' Patrick said, and Joe turned his head, gave an unexpected grin and led Patrick round to the far side of Camden's big four-wheel drive, parked next to the pub dustbins. He knelt down, fiddled with the valve cap and Patrick heard the hiss of escaping air. Joe obviously knew who the real culprit was. He then went round to the windscreen and wrote, in mirror writing on the dirt, *CHECK YOUR TYRES*. Then he slapped Patrick on the back and mimed walking with his fingers.

'You want us to go for a walk?' Patrick asked.

The other man nodded and set off into the darkness.

It was soon obvious it was to be no mere stroll. Joe's long stride took them rapidly through the churchyard, over a stile and down the side of the field beyond. They took an old overgrown pathway down through the wood to the lower ground by the river and climbed another stile onto a signposted path. They walked fast for an hour and a half without ever taking to a road.

Joe climbed a wall and on the far side stretched his hand out to stop Patrick from blundering into a barbed-wire fence, hidden by darkness and foliage. The wood ahead looked impenetrably gloomy and Patrick said, a little nervously, 'Where are we going?' but Joe had already gone on into the wood on a narrow twisting track.

After many minutes they came to a bank and climbed down it to a wider track, surfaced with gravel and rough stones. The track curved and ran downhill for a hundred yards, and then in the darkness, rising above them, Patrick made out dim cliffs of rock and guessed they had arrived at a quarry.

Joe took him to the far end of it, picking his way between piles of old tyres and mounds of rubble, then crouched down, took a little torch out of his pocket and shone it on the ground, waving to Patrick to come and look. What they were looking at was the edge of a huge pile of earth. Small fragments of colour glinted in the torchlight, Roman tesserae, tumbled into the heap of soil that had been dragged there from Little's field. All they amounted to now was useless builder's rubble.

'My God, what a waste,' Patrick said, turning to Joe. 'Have you been out searching for this every night?'

He got a single emphatic nod.

'Well done, Joe. We need to come and check through this lot. It won't do much good, though. We'll never prove it was him, will we?'

Joe nodded two or three times.

'We will? How? You've got proof?'

Joe shone the torch on himself and passed it to Patrick like that, then, smiling, he held out his hands as in a game of charades, making the symbols for book, film and play in quick succession.

Patrick laughed. 'You're going to act it?'

There was a quick nod.

'Two words. First word?'

Joe brought his two hands close together.

'Small? Something like small?' Joe was encouraging him. 'Oh, got it. Little? Yes. Second word?'

Joe stuck his arms out, tilting and making a droning noise.

'Aeroplane?'

Joe egged him on, then mimed, with a flat hand, something curving down to a horizontal halt.

'Aeroplane landing? Yes? Yes. Landing. Shorter than landing. Land? OK, land. That's it? Little land. What? Little's land? He owns this place? You're kidding.'

Joe mimed somebody taking aim with a gun and firing.

'He keeps it for shooting? And you knew that so you came and searched? Oh, bloody well done, mate. We'll get him now.'

It was one o'clock in the morning before they were back in the village and Patrick, completely exhausted, waved good night to Joe.

CD woke him in the morning. 'Hate to wake you but we've got a tiny little rebellion on our hands.'

'I found where Little dumped the stuff. Joe showed me.'

'Good, good. There's something more important than that going on. Or, rather, not going on.'

'Like what?'

'Like breakfast.'

A NOTE WAS PINNED to the flap of the marquee. It said: *Milk and bread inside. Make your own breakfast. I've had to go. Pub will do lunch if you tell them you're coming. Maybe supper. B.*

'This is all about me,' said Patrick, reading it ruefully.

'Yeah, I know. She was pretty angry last night after you guys went out. She had a go at Camden too,' said CD. 'It was not nice to hear.'

'I'll go down and see her.'

'I wouldn't go in without back-up, the way she sounded,' said CD. 'Take Dozer. Well, no. Normally that would be a good plan but he's otherwise occupied.' CD turned and stared at Dozer's tent.

'How?'

As if in answer, the zip opened and a face looked out, but it wasn't Dozer. Seeing them staring, it vanished again.

'Gaye? Was that Gaye?' said Patrick. 'No, it couldn't have been.'

'Believe it, baby. It's that end of the dig, last days of Rome atmosphere. They decided last night they were made for each other. In different factories maybe, but there you go.'

'I've got to go down and sort this out with Bobby. She thinks I tricked Joe into being filmed.'

But at the farmhouse there was just another note on the door. It said: *Louisa. I've gone to the Citizens' Advice Bureau. The hearing's at ten thirty at Oxford court. See you there. B.*

Patrick's mobile rang as he read it.

'Patrick. It's John Hescroft. Look, Kenny Camden asked me to give you a call. Can we meet at the conservation lab in twenty minutes? They've got some of your stuff from the trench cleaned up for the cameras and Jack's going to shoot some pictures. I thought it was a good chance for us to fly the PSC corporate flag a bit.'

Patrick almost laughed. He'd known Hescroft would pop up when the hard work was done and try to get his face on the programme. 'OK,' he said. 'I need to talk to Camden anyway, but listen, John. There's something else. Last night we found the soil that was stripped from the Roman site dumped on a bit of private land belonging to Roger Little. Can you tell the council?'

'Oh, that's a dead duck, surely?'

'No, it isn't. Will you tell them or will I?'

'It's very embarrassing, Patrick. I see him at the golf club.'

'You've got a conflict of interests?'

'Oh, no. No, no. Nothing like that. Talk about it later, old boy. I'll see you at the laboratory.'

Kenny Camden and Jack were waiting with the camera gear in the foyer of the lab. Patrick walked right up close to Camden.

'I'd like to know what you think you were doing last night?

'Well, I had an excellent meal at the Luna Caprese, then—'

'In the pub.'

'We were filming, Pat. Perfectly within our rights. We had the landlady's permission.'

'You didn't have Joe's permission.'

'Didn't need it. He was performing on her premises under her licence. That puts her in charge.'

Patrick had no idea whether he was right or not. 'Well, I'm not having this. It's dishonest. You sent Joe the note, didn't you? You pretended it was me asking him to sing?'

'I might ask *you* who let down my tyre?'

At that moment, John Hescroft came in, spraying a foam of oblivious false bonhomie on the flames.

'Morning, old boy. Hello, Jack.' He looked at each of them in turn, frowning. 'Is there a problem?' he asked.

'Forget it,' said Patrick. 'What happened with the council?'

'I left a message. We'll have to see. If you've really got proof they might go for a prosecution.'

'Will it affect the planning permission?'

'Separate issue, I would have thought. Not really my bailiwick, nor yours, come to think of it. Perhaps we'd better stick to the job in hand. Paul McGovern should be expecting us. Let's give him a shout.'

McGovern, a ponderous man, came out to meet them and led them into a side room where various familiar objects were laid out on a table, dominated by the sword.

'We've finished all the cleaning,' he said.

Patrick leaned over the sword, studying it intently.

'This is very fine,' said Hescroft, joining him, 'very fine indeed.'

Patrick ran through a mental check list. The coins were there and the shield boss . . . The heavy disc of Roman work was missing.

'There's something else,' he said.

'I was saving that for last,' McGovern said. 'I think you'll like this. It's cleaned up very nicely.'

He lifted a plastic cover and an astonishing sight was revealed. What Patrick had only seen as an encrusted lump was now a disc of bronze, with an intricately cast man's face at its centre, perforated with holes at intervals all across it. Patrick knew this face already—the face of a man with a beard made up of leaves and fruit, and with two birds flying out of his mouth, a face later carved in wood and central to a tradition kept alive down the years to the present day. A tradition that was about to be put through the processes of modern law.

'Um, I need to borrow this for an hour or two.'

'What for?' demanded Camden, as Patrick picked it up. 'Where are you going? We need you. We need to get pictures of that.'

'I'll be back. Phone me on the mobile when you finish here. I'll join you.' Then he was gone.

'What was that about?' said Camden. 'Can anyone tell me why—' He snapped his fingers. 'Bloody hell, I know what it is. It's Joe's sister. It's about her court case this morning, I bet. Come on, Jack. We'll shoot this later. First things first.'

By that time, Patrick was already starting his engine. He drove into Oxford as fast as the traffic would allow. It took far too long to find a parking space and further agonising minutes to find out where Bobby's hearing was taking place. When he finally walked into the courtroom, it was already well under way.

A barrister in wig and gown was addressing the judge. His every syllable sounded expensive. '. . . in accordance with that. It is therefore the contention of the governors of the school in seeking this injunction that the parade is not in fact an old tradition at all and that there is no record which can be produced in evidence of any such tradition going back before the Second World War.'

Patrick couldn't spot Bobby to start with, then he realised she was the woman in unfamiliar smart clothes and a hat like a turban, who was sitting at the front of the court. He started scribbling her a note. But it was too late to get it to her. She was already standing up to speak.

'In the village, we know it's been going for years and years,' she said, 'since time immemorial.' It sounded vague and he knew instantly that it wouldn't wash. What could he do?

In a corner, at the back of the chamber, was a large whiteboard and felt-tip pen. He went to it and wrote in big block letters, *BOBBY, CALL ME AS A WITNESS*. Bobby didn't turn round. The judge was now looking at him over his glasses.

'Miss Redhead,' said the judge, 'a young man at the back of the court appears to be attempting to attract your attention.'

Bobby twisted round sharply and finally took in Patrick and his message.

'Do you know what this is about?' the judge asked her.

'No, Your Honour, I don't,' said Bobby. 'The, er . . . the young man is an archaeologist.'

Patrick saw the vicar, the head teacher and Roger Little, complete with a bruise just under his eye, frowning.

'He is perhaps an expert on local history?' suggested the judge.

'Perhaps,' said Bobby vaguely. 'I don't, well, I'm not sure . . .'

'May I suggest you call him as an expert witness? You do seem a little, well, undersupported,' said the judge kindly, so she did.

Patrick went to sit in the witness box and she stared at him, unable to tell what he could be doing there.

'You are Patrick Kane,' she said, 'an archaeologist who has been digging on an Anglo-Saxon burial site in the village of Wytchlow?'

'Yes, I am.'

'And . . .' There was a long silence, and he tried to get her to notice the bronze disc he was holding but her eyes were fixed above it, staring at his face. 'And,' she said decisively, 'what question would you like me to ask you?'

'I'd like you to ask me about the disc-shaped Roman artefact that we discovered buried in the Anglo-Saxon grave.'

'Mr Kane,' she said, 'would you tell us about the, er . . . the disc-shaped Roman thing?'

He held it up and she finally focused on it and her eyes widened.

'Yes,' he said, 'as you have no doubt already told the court, the May Day procession centres on the parade round the village of an old Bath chair carrying a very distinctive wooden mask in the shape of a Green Man face with two birds flying out of the mouth. The issue seems to be whether this has or has not been a long tradition. While we were digging in the Anglo-Saxon grave at Wytchlow, we discovered this Roman object buried with the body. The object was obscured by an encrustation of dirt, but I have just collected it from the laboratories where it has been cleaned. It is possible to date it with a high degree of confidence to the third or fourth century.'

He looked across at the vicar, who had his mouth tightly shut, then turned to the judge. 'It is virtually identical to the wooden mask used in the parade. I would infer, Your Honour, that there must be a very ancient tradition based around this particular facial form.'

IN THE CORRIDOR OUTSIDE, Patrick expected Bobby to be grateful for his Lone Ranger act, riding to her rescue at the last moment, but her anger ran deep.

'I suppose you think that was clever, crashing in like that,' she said. 'And I suppose you think it makes up for your truly disgusting behaviour over Joe. Well, it doesn't.' She walked off towards the WAY OUT sign.

Patrick went to follow her but his phone rang. Two of the Wytchlow mothers who had been in the court stood there looking at him with sheeplike admiration. At least he'd pleased somebody. Hescroft's voice in his ear said, 'Where are you?'

'In town.'

'Look, do pull yourself together. There's a change of plan.

Kenny and Jack had to shoot off. Will you nip along to Celia Longworth at the computer place? She was expecting all of us. Can you give her a message? Camden wants her to bring the face reconstruction stuff out to Wytchlow on a laptop this afternoon so we can film all the village people looking at it.'

'Where is it?' Patrick said wearily.

'Thirteen, Mortlake Street,' said Hescroft. 'Get your skates on.' He hung up.

'Do you know where Mortlake Street is?' Patrick asked the two women.

'I think it's off the Iffley Road,' said one. 'Just after a pub.'

ON THE WAY, Patrick hissed at the windscreen all the things that he wished he'd said to Bobby. 'You ask your brother who got him to sing. He'll tell you. Somehow. You go off like a bloody firework all the time. Well, I've had it. Go back to your bloody farming and leave me alone. I'm glad the dig's nearly over. You're so ungrateful. You've got your bloody parade and that's down to me. How could I do it any other way? You think you're so brave about life and I'm so spineless. Well, you don't know me at all. Get out of my bloody way.'

He blew his horn at a cyclist who'd done nothing worse than travel on roughly the same bit of tarmac.

Then he thought instead of the other woman, the German Queen. She was so much easier to understand. He could safely let himself feel things for her that were far too powerful to be turned on anyone alive. She was a brave, straightforward woman, and he let himself love the idea of her. She had commanded love. That was what the tributes they'd piled round her said. And in a few minutes he would see her face. The impact of that hit him. He knew that it was all he needed—the sight of her face—to complete what he knew about her from the song and from the feel of her bones in the soil.

At 13 Mortlake Street, Celia Longworth took him to an upstairs room where three tables were crammed with a mass of monitors, keyboards and cabling. A young man was working at one of them. His hair was streaked blond and he had two silver rings in one ear.

'This is Nick,' said Celia. 'He's my right-hand man. Nick, this is Patrick. He's come to see his Saxon woman.'

'Great,' said the youth, then he did a double take. 'Patrick?'

'Yes, that's right,' Patrick said firmly.

But Nick kept staring at him. 'I know you, don't I?'

'Someone's party, maybe?' said Patrick. 'Do you know Alice?'

'Yeah, Alice. Was it there?'

It seemed to work. Patrick filed that one away for future use.

'This is where we do the clever stuff,' Celia explained. 'Now, do you know how all this works?'

'Vaguely.'

'The skull gives the face about ninety-five per cent of its shape, of course, but it's the other five per cent that matters, and that comes from the soft tissue, the muscle and the flesh. That's what's tough to get just right. Get the soft tissue wrong and you wouldn't recognise your own mother. Can you put up the skull, Nick?'

On a huge monitor, the familiar scanned-in skull of the woman from Wytchlow came up, slowly revolving, to reveal the great jagged hole across one side.

'There's our starting point. We'll just fix the damage.'

Keys clicked and the skull healed over.

'In the old days, the big problems were the mouth, the nose and the ears. No one could be sure of any of that. Now we've learned how to work most of it out from looking really closely at how the muscles attach. The marks on the skull tell us which way they pulled and how strongly.'

She was an enthusiast lost in the wonders of her world. All Patrick wanted to see was the outcome.

'If the teeth are still there, the outer edge of the canines gives you the width of the mouth and that also tells you exactly how the eyes were set because it's the same as the width between the inner edges of the iris. The general shape of the nose is quite easy. Do you want me to explain that?'

'No, I've got the general idea.'

'OK. Nick, give me the average face.'

On the screen a flattened mask appeared and wrapped itself over the skull. It looked like a shop-window dummy.

'Right, that's using average soft-tissue depths superimposed on the skull. Now the clever bit with this software is that we've built in different average values for various ethnic groups. So now we'll try with Saxon averages.'

'How do you get Saxon averages?'

'By going to Saxony,' she said, as if it ought to be obvious.

The face that formed on the screen, after Nick had added some brown hair, was blandly beautiful, but it didn't look at all like someone who would have picked up her father's sword.

'She doesn't look the hero type,' Patrick said, and Celia laughed. 'Of course she might have been the result of intermarriage,' he went on. 'Her mother could have been a Briton. We have no real idea.'

'I could do you a bit of Celt,' said Nick, and got busy on the keyboard, calling up menus onto his screen. 'I'll try sixty-forty Celt and Saxon, yes? What about a bit of heroic red hair for the full Celtic experience?'

'OK.'

It took a little while to process, the screen flickering as a new face emerged. This one took Patrick's breath away. The song had come to life before his eyes.

'Oh yes,' he said. 'Oh yes, that's her. That's definitely her.'

He felt absurdly happy, absurdly hopeful. This was the woman so valiant that she had been given the privilege of a warrior's burial. They had retrieved her from oblivion.

'How about that?' said Nick. 'Isn't she just something?'

'That's sixty-forty, is it, Nick?' said Celia. 'Try it forty-sixty.'

'No,' said Patrick vehemently. He couldn't bear to lose her.

'OK,' said Celia. 'Now, do you want to see her walk?'

The wonderful woman on the screen moved down a stylised country lane and began to walk towards them with a swinging, athletic stride. Was that a suggested bulge of pregnancy? It was extremely lifelike and Patrick gazed at her, lost in love. Nick pressed another button and she began to run with her hair flowing out behind her.

'Did you see how she threw her weight forward when she ran?' said Nick proudly. 'It's all from the joint and muscle marking analysis.'

'Now the really clever bit,' Celia added, 'is that we've managed to analyse the force and the direction of the blow that caused the damage to the skull. It was probably a single-edged weapon struck downwards and from behind, something like this.'

Then, before Patrick could prepare himself for it in any way, the woman appeared again, but this time she was being overtaken by a huge man with a blade raised behind him, a blade that slashed down into the side of her head as she came close. It was intensely realistic. Patrick cried out as the German Queen collapsed. He found his eyes flooding with tears.

'No,' he said, choked, and lunged for the door.

'Are you all right,' Celia called out, but he ran down the stairs and out onto the pavement, overflowing with illogical grief.

He heard someone shout his name and there, coming down the pavement towards him, was Bobby. She broke into a run and a gust of wind took away her turban, releasing the hair he had never seen before in daylight, a cascade of deep red curls that tumbled around her lively, living face. She was so like the picture he had just seen on the screen that he searched the pavement behind her, heart pounding, looking for the giant swordsman.

She stopped in front of him and looked at him quizzically. 'What's happened to you?'

'Everything.' He hugged her.

'Wow. What's this for?' she gasped.

'For being alive,' he said, and kissed her hard.

She went tense for a moment, then kissed him back. When she broke away, breathing hard, she looked at him wonderingly and said, 'Jack told me it wasn't you.'

'How did you find me?'

'You asked Louisa where thirteen Mortlake Street was. Patrick, I need you. Jack says they're going back to Wytchlow to corner Joe. Jack can't stand Camden. He says Camden gave Joe a note this morning saying that if he didn't do the song, they'd do all the stuff about you instead. He thinks Joe's going to agree to sing.'

'Well, let's go and stop him, shall we?'

In the car, he looked sideways at her.

'I can't believe I haven't seen your hair properly before,' he said. 'Why do you always wear that horrible cap?'

'That's just a farmer thing,' she said dismissively, trying to scoop it all up and put the turban back on. It got out of control and she let it all tumble down again. 'Well, actually, can you imagine what it's like to be called Redhead and have hair like this?'

'Rather wonderful I should say.' He could hardly drag his eyes away.

'Watch the road. Does this thing go any faster? You look nice when you smile.'

'I'll do it more often.' He took her hand.

'Don't you need to change gear or anything?'

'Only sometimes.'

'What on earth happened inside that building? Was it the DNA results? Why did you come rushing out like that?'

'It was the face reconstruction. You'll see it later on. Forget the DNA. It takes ages. I'll tell you something, though.' He looked at her and a warm glow of certainty about the future flooded his body. 'There's not much point in waiting for it. I know the results already.'

He wouldn't tell her any more.

As they tore into Bobby's farmyard they were greeted by an unexpected scene. A grinning Joe, carrying a guitar, waved cheerfully. Camden, looking like he'd lost his wallet, was scrawling something on a clipboard while Jack, whistling aimlessly, folded his tripod.

'They've done it,' said Bobby. 'We're too late.'

They got out of the car and Jack winked at them.

'What's happened?' demanded Bobby.

'I've just wasted the last hour, that's what's happened,' said Camden. 'I suppose everyone thought it was very funny.'

'Do you want to see it?' said Jack. 'I can run it back through the viewfinder.'

'Yeah, that's right, let them have their laugh,' said Camden, and he climbed inside his car.

Jack ran the videotape back for them. Bobby and Patrick shared the headphones, their cheeks touching.

The camera showed Joe in the yard, washing off his boots with a hosepipe.

'Mr Redhead?' said Camden's voice.

Joe looked up and smiled.

'Could we have a word?' said Camden. 'Actually, I understand it's difficult to have a word because you don't speak at all.'

Joe looked surprised, shrugged, then said perfectly clearly, if a little slowly, 'Well, whoever could have told you that, I wonder?'

Camden, out of shot, seemed to have been struck dumb himself, and Joe waited, then asked politely, 'Was there anything else?'

Camden said, 'Er . . . there was a song you sang in the pub. The one about the German Queen. Would you sing it for us?'

'Oh well, you see I make them up as I go along. Can't say I remember that one. I have got one song I can do for you.'

'Er . . . all right,' said Camden.

'Wait a minute.'

There was a long pause while Joe disappeared into the house. The camera stayed on and they could hear Camden, off-mike, say, 'I think someone's been pulling my plonker.'

Joe came back with his guitar, tuned up and launched into a basic folk melody.

'There's a man they call Little who lives in this village,
And all that he's good for is plunder and pillage.
When they came to dig up what the Romans had left
He saw a threat to his profits so he turned to theft.

For the past it is yours and the past it is mine
And the man that destroys it is naught but a swine.
He brought lorries and bulldozers late in the night
And he wrecked the old villa as he dug up that site.

He'll make a small fortune as he sells off each house
That won't change the fact that he's simply a louse
For the past it is yours and the past it is mine
And the man that destroys it is naught but a swine.'

'Did you like that?' said Joe to the camera. There was no reply.

Jack stopped the film. 'That's it,' he said. 'Deeply satisfying.'

Patrick followed Bobby into the kitchen where Joe was standing by the Aga, waiting for the kettle to boil.

Bobby hugged him. 'You old bastard. How did you do that? Come on, say something to me.'

But Joe just smiled and put a finger to his lips. Then he took Bobby's hand, led her over to Patrick and wrapped Patrick's hand round hers. He kissed Bobby on the forehead and left the room.

'Ah,' said Bobby, 'that's odd. I seem to have just been . . . well . . . *given* to you, I suppose. Not even gift-wrapped.'

'The wrapping's perfect,' said Patrick, running his fingers through her hair and pulling her gently towards him.

THE NEXT MORNING, Patrick woke in a soft bed with his arms wrapped round Bobby. She was smiling into his eyes with a hint of wonder and he knew his penance was over.

'Hello,' he said. 'It wasn't a dream, then?'

She kissed him. 'Time to get up,' she said. 'It's May Morning.'

They walked out into the freshest day of Patrick's life and took the lane to the meadow by the river. There were families converging on it from every direction, small children running ahead to pick flowers out of the hedges. Bobby took a small bottle from her pocket and together they knelt down to gather dew from the grass.

They joined the children in gathering armfuls of flowers then trooped back from the field to decorate the cart.

It was then that Patrick remembered the priceless bronze object he had left in the car the day before. 'Would your wooden man mind if his ancestor took his place round the village this year?'

'Why don't they both come?'

So they wove the flower stems into the holes in the face of the bronze man and then, with the May Queen crowned, Patrick and Bobby took their place in the procession.

FIVE MONTHS LATER, the diggers gathered on the hilltop to bury the German Queen and her child again, laying the bones out tenderly just as they had found them. After a series of heated debates in Oxford, they had given up hope of reburying most of the grave goods with her, but Bobby insisted when it came to the Green Man mask. 'I know how she felt about it,' she said. The mask was carefully copied and the original face went quietly back into the grave.

Jack arrived by himself, with no camera, and asked if he might join them. They buried the bones with enormous care, sieving the heap of fine soil down over them, then they rolled the turf carefully back into place over the grave and laid flowers down.

The tents blossomed again in their old places and, with the campfire blazing and wine bottles being passed round, it was what they all wanted, a re-creation of past times, except now, as Dozer said, lying with his arm round Gaye, it seemed a whole lot nicer.

They talked for a while about the amazing moment when they had first seen the reconstruction.

'I was sure they were going to find your DNA was the same as hers,' said Gaye to Bobby. 'They must have got it wrong.'

'Not necessarily,' said Peter. 'It could go all the way down the line to Bobby's grandmother, then if it came down her father's side instead of her mother's it wouldn't show up, see?'

'Well, *we* all know who she's descended from, don't we?' said Gaye, and Patrick agreed.

'What did you think of the programme?' said Jack diffidently.

'Could have been worse,' said CD. 'I was glad to see Camden let old Patrick here off lightly. All it really said was that you used to be a rock singer and now you weren't.'

'Funny that,' said Jack. 'Bit of a technical problem with some of the videotapes. I don't suppose I'll be working for him again.'

'Well, it's past history now,' said Patrick.

'Can you tell us what happened about Roger Little?' asked Aidan. 'I couldn't help noticing there hasn't been any building on the field.'

'The Woodland Renewal Trust bought it,' said Bobby.

'So did he not get his planning permission then?'

'Yes, he did. Then he sold up. It's all a bit of a mystery.'

'No, it's not,' said Dozer, too far away for Patrick to kick him into silence. 'I made him an offer he couldn't refuse.'

'What with?' said Bobby in amazement. 'I didn't know that.'

'Spare royalties some pop star had hanging around, weren't it, Pat? Mind you, I got it for a rock-bottom price, having all that evidence of Roman flooring. He saw my point of view quite quickly, really. I was quite reasonable.'

‘Where’s Joe gone?’ asked Maxwell. ‘I didn’t see him go.’

‘He was here,’ said Bobby. ‘I think he went down to the barn. Have you seen it? He’s made a great job of it. Patrick and I said he didn’t have to move out just for us but you can’t argue with him.’

‘Well, you could, but it might be a bit one-sided,’ said Dozer. ‘Here he is.’

Joe walked up out of the darkness with two guitars and gave one to Patrick. They made space for him in the circle.

‘There’s only one song I want to hear tonight,’ said Bobby, resting her head on Patrick’s shoulder, and there under the stars, the two guitars met in perfect understanding, and Joe sang the whole story to its sweet finale.

JAMES LONG

How does a BBC economics correspondent and one-time student of car design end up writing a novel about Anglo-Saxon relics? James Long can't fully explain this surprising contrast of interests, but does remember a key turning point in his career, marked by John Birt's arrival at the BBC—'Let's just say there was a certain incompatibility about our approaches'. So, in 1988, after many years spent covering business and political stories around the globe, he cut loose and, with a friend, set up an independent TV channel showing European business programmes. When it went 'spectacularly bankrupt' after two years, he found himself free to do what he'd always wanted to do—write novels.

James Long's first four books were political thrillers, but with the publication in 1988 of *Ferney*, a novel about a woman reunited with a lover from a past life, he turned his hand to a far more romantic kind of story. *Silence and Shadows*, in fact, stemmed from a conversation he had with a friend, a retired archaeologist who lived in the Oxfordshire area where the novel is set. 'He was amazing. You could go field-walking with him and every so often he'd kick a lump of earth and pick up a bronze brooch or a piece of Roman tile. He'd been on a dig once where they'd found a female burial. Because of worries about grave robbers, he had to move his camp bed over the grave and sleep there at night, literally inches above the skeleton. In the course of the dig, he felt that he'd formed a bond with the unknown woman that was stronger, in some ways, than many human relationships he'd had.'

James Long lives in Devon with his wife and three children. He wishes now that he'd studied archaeology while at university. 'I got to take part in a dig in the course of researching *Silence and Shadows* and it was just fantastic. I'll be doing it again.'

201-012